D0599544

When Christmas Comes

Christmas 2004

Dear Reader,

My fascination with romantic comedies set during the Christmas
season continues. With all the stress of preparing for the holidays,
I feel we all need a reason to laugh. So, my friend, I'd like to encourage
you to settle in your most comfortable chair, pour yourself a cup of
Christmas cheer and read *When Christmas Comes.*

I do promise you'll laugh at what happens when two people decide
to trade homes over Christmas. Throw a Christmas curmudgeon into
a town obsessed with Christmas, then add meddling neighborhood
children and a hungry goat. For good measure, there's a troupe of
actors, a daughter who's run off with her boyfriend, and a widow
stuck alone in a city where she doesn't know a solitary person. Add to
the mix the spark of romance, budding friendships and an interfering
mother who would do just about anything to marry off her bachelor
sons. You get the picture.

Does that sound like fun, or what? I do hope you'll enjoy
When Christmas Comes. May you laugh and fall in love all
over again and look at the Christmas season in a whole new way.

Debbie Macomber

P.S. Be sure to check out my Web page at www.debbiemacomber.com.
I enjoy getting feedback from my readers. If you aren't online, I can be
reached at P.O. Box 1458, Port Orchard, WA 98366.

DEBBIE MACOMBER

When Christmas Comes

MIRA®

ISBN 0-7783-2090-1

WHEN CHRISTMAS COMES

Copyright © 2004 by Debbie Macomber.

All rights reserved. Except for use in any review, the reproduction or utilization of this work in whole or in part in any form by any electronic, mechanical or other means, now known or hereafter invented, including xerography, photocopying and recording, or in any information storage or retrieval system, is forbidden without the written permission of the publisher, MIRA Books, 225 Duncan Mill Road, Don Mills, Ontario, Canada M3B 3K9.

All characters in this book have no existence outside the imagination of the author and have no relation whatsoever to anyone bearing the same name or names. They are not even distantly inspired by any individual known or unknown to the author, and all incidents are pure invention.

MIRA and the Star Colophon are trademarks used under license and registered in Australia, New Zealand, Philippines, United States Patent and Trademark Office and in other countries.

www.MIRABooks.com

Printed in U.S.A.

First Printing: November 2004
10 9 8 7 6 5 4 3 2 1

For my cousin Paula Bearson, with gratitude.
And special thanks to writer and friend Ann DeFee.

Chapter One

"What do you mean you won't be home for Christmas?" Emily Springer was sure she couldn't have heard correctly. She pressed the telephone receiver harder against her ear, as though that would clarify her daughter's words.

"Mom, I know you're disappointed...."

That didn't even begin to cover it. Emily had scraped and sacrificed in order to save airfare home for her only daughter, a student at Harvard. They always spent the holidays together, and now Heather was telling her she wouldn't be back for Christmas.

"What could possibly be more important than Christmas with your family?" Emily asked, struggling to hide her distress.

Her daughter hesitated. "It's just that I've got so much going on during those two weeks. I'd love to be home with you, I really would, but...I can't."

Emily swallowed past the lump in her throat. Heather was twenty-one; Emily realized her daughter was becoming an independent adult, but for the last eleven years it had been just the two of them. The thought of being separated from her only child over Christmas brought tears to her eyes.

"You've got all the neighbor kids to spoil," Heather continued.

Yes, the six Kennedy children would be more than happy to gobble up Emily's homemade cookies, candies and other traditional holiday treats. But it wouldn't be the same.

"I was home a few months ago," Heather reminded her next.

Emily opened her mouth to argue. True, her daughter had spent the summer in Leavenworth, but she'd been busy working and saving money for school. If she wasn't at her library job, she was with her friends. Emily knew that Heather had her own life now, her own friends, her own priorities and plans. That was to be expected and natural, and Emily told herself she should be proud. But spending Christmas on opposite sides of the country was simply too hard—especially for the two of them, who'd once been so close.

"What about the money I saved for your airfare?" Emily asked lamely, as if that would change anything.

"I'll fly out for Easter, Mom. I'll use it then."

Easter was months away, and Emily didn't know if she could last that long. This was dreadful. Three weeks before Christmas, and she'd lost every shred of holiday spirit.

"I have to hang up now, Mom."

"I know, but...can't we talk about this? I mean, there's got to be a way for us to be together."

Heather hesitated once more. "You'll be fine without me."

"Of course I will," Emily said, dredging up the remnants of her pride. The last thing she wanted was to look pathetic to her daughter—or to heap on the guilt—so she spoke with an enthusiasm she didn't feel. Disappointment pounded through her with every beat of her heart. She had to remember she wasn't the only one who'd be alone, though. Heather would be missing out, too. "What about you?" Emily asked. Caught up in her own distress, she hadn't been thinking about her daughter's feelings. "Will you be all alone?"

"For Christmas, you mean?" Heather said. Her voice fell slightly, and it sounded as if she too was putting on a brave front. "I have friends here, and I'll probably get together with them—but it won't be the same."

That had been Emily's reaction: *It won't be the same.* This Christmas marked the beginning of a new stage in their relationship. It was inevitable—but Christmas was still Christmas, and she vowed that wherever Heather was in future years, they'd spend the holiday together. Emily squared her shoulders. "We'll make it through this," she said stoutly.

"Of course we will."

"I'll be in touch soon," Emily promised.

"I knew you'd be a trouper about this, Mom."

Heather actually seemed proud of her, but Emily was no heroine. After a brief farewell, she placed the portable phone back in the charger and slumped into the closest chair.

Moping around, Emily tried to fight off a sense of depression that had begun to descend. She couldn't concentrate on anything, too restless to read or watch TV. The house felt...bleak. Uncharacteristically so. Maybe because she hadn't put up the Christmas decorations, knowing how much Heather loved helping her.

They had their own traditions. Heather always decorated the fireplace mantel, starting with her favorite piece, a small almost-antique angel that had belonged to Emily's mother. While she did that, Emily worked on the windowsills around the dining room, arranging garlands, candles and poinsettias. Then together, using the ornaments Emily had collected over the years, they'd decorate the Christmas tree. Not an artificial one, either, despite warnings that they were safer than fresh trees.

It sometimes took them half a day to choose their Christmas tree. Leavenworth was a small Washington town tucked in the foothills of the Cascade Mountains, and it offered a stunning array of firs and pines.

This year, without Heather, there would be no tree. Emily wouldn't bother. Really, why go to that much effort when she'd be the only one there to enjoy it. Why decorate the house at all?

This Christmas was destined to be her worst since Peter had died. Her husband had been killed in a logging accident eleven years earlier. Before his death, her life had been idyllic—exactly what she'd wanted it to be. They'd been high-school sweethearts and married the summer after graduation. From the start, their marriage was close and companionable. A year later Heather had arrived. Peter had supported Emily's efforts to obtain her teaching degree and they'd postponed adding to their family. The three of them had been contented, happy with their little household—and then, overnight, her entire world had collapsed.

Peter's life insurance had paid for the funeral and allowed her to deal with the financial chaos. Emily had invested the funds wisely; she'd also continued with her job as a kindergarten teacher. She and Heather were as close as a mother and daughter could be. In her heart, Emily knew Peter would have been so proud of Heather.

The scholarship to Harvard was well deserved but it wasn't enough to meet all of Heather's expenses. Emily periodically cashed in some of her investments to pay her daughter's living costs— her dorm room, her transportation, her textbooks and entertainment. Emily lived frugally, and her one and only extravagance was Christmas. For the last two years, they'd somehow managed to be together even though Heather had moved to Boston. Now this...

Still overwhelmed by her disappointment, Emily wandered into the study and stared at the blank computer screen. Her friend Faith would understand how she felt. Faith would give her the sympathy she needed. They communicated frequently via e-mail. Although Faith was ten years younger, they'd become good friends. They were both teachers; Faith had done her student teaching in Leavenworth and they'd stayed in touch.

Faith—braver than Emily—taught junior high literature. Emily cringed at the thought of not only facing a hundred thirteen-year-olds every school day but trying to interest them in things like poetry. Divorced for the past five years, Faith lived in the Oakland Bay area of San Francisco.

This news about Heather's change in plans couldn't be delivered by e-mail, Emily decided. She needed immediate comfort. She needed Faith to assure her that she could get through the holidays by herself.

She reached for the phone and hit speed dial for Faith's number. Her one hope was that Faith would be home on a Sunday afternoon—and to Emily's relief, Faith snatched up the receiver after the second ring.

"Hi! It's Emily," she said, doing her best to sound cheerful.

"What's wrong?"

How well Faith knew her. In a flood of emotion, Emily spilled out everything Heather had told her.

"She's got a boyfriend," Faith announced as if it were a foregone conclusion.

"Well, she has mentioned a boy named Ben a few times, but the relationship doesn't sound serious."

"Don't you believe it!"

Faith tended to be something of a cynic, especially when it came to relationships. Emily didn't blame her; Faith had married her college boyfriend and stayed in the marriage for five miserable years.

She'd moved to Leavenworth shortly after her divorce. Her connection with Emily had been forged during a time of loneliness, and they'd each found solace in their friendship.

"I'm sure Heather would tell me if this had to do with a man in her life," Emily said fretfully, "but she didn't say one word. It's school and work and all the pressures. I understand, or at least I'm trying to, but I feel so…so cheated."

"Those are just excuses. Trust me, there's a man involved."

Not wanting to accept it but unwilling to argue the point, Emily sighed deeply. "Boyfriend or not," she muttered, "I'll be alone over the holidays. How can I possibly celebrate Christmas by myself?"

Faith laughed—which Emily didn't consider very sympathetic. "All you have to do is look out your front window."

That was true enough. Leavenworth was about as close to Santa's village as any place could get. The entire town entered the Christmas spirit. Tourists from all over the country visited the small community, originally founded by immigrants from Germany, and marveled at its festive atmosphere. Every year there were train rides and Christmas-tree-lighting ceremonies, three in all, plus winter sports and sleigh rides and Christmas parades and more.

Emily's home was sixty years old and one block from the heart of downtown. The city park was across the street. Starting in early December, groups of carolers strolled through the neighborhood dressed in old-fashioned regalia. With the horse-drawn sleigh, and groups of men and women in greatcoats and long dresses gathered under streetlamps, the town looked like a Currier & Ives print.

"Everyone else can be in the holiday spirit, but I won't—not without Heather," Emily said. "I'm not even going to put up a tree."

"You don't mean that," Faith told her bracingly.

"I do so," Emily insisted. She couldn't imagine anything that would salvage Christmas for her.

"What you need is a shot of holiday cheer. Watch *Miracle on 34th Street* or—"

"It won't help," Emily cried. "Nothing will."

"Emily, this doesn't sound like you. Besides," Faith said, "Heather's twenty-one. She's creating her own life, and that's completely appropriate. So she can't make it this year—you'll have *next* Christmas with her."

Emily didn't respond. She couldn't think of anything to say.

"You need your own life, too," Faith added. "I've been after you for years to join the church singles group."

"I'll join when you do," Emily returned.

"Might I remind you that I no longer live in Leavenworth?"

"Fine, join one in Oakland."

"That's not the point, Em," her friend said. "You've been so wrapped up in Heather that you don't have enough going on in *your* life."

"You know that's not true!" Emily could see that talking to Faith wasn't having the desired effect. "I called because I need sympathy," Emily said, her tone a bit petulant even to her own ears.

Faith laughed softly. "I've failed you, then."

"Yes." Emily figured she might as well tell the truth. "Of all people, I thought you'd understand."

"I'm sorry to disappoint you, Em."

Her friend didn't *sound* sorry.

"I actually think being apart over the holidays might be good for you—and for Heather."

Emily was aghast that Faith would suggest such a thing. "How can you say that?"

"Heather might appreciate you more and you might just discover that there are other possibilities at Christmas than spending it with your daughter."

Emily knew she'd adjust much more easily if she wasn't a widow. Being alone at this time of year was hard, had been hard ever since Peter's death. Perhaps Faith was right. Perhaps she'd clung to her daughter emotionally, but Emily felt that in her circumstances, it was forgivable.

"I'll be fine," she managed, but she didn't believe it for a moment.

"I know you will," Faith said.

Even more distressed than before, Emily finished the conversation and hung up the phone. Never having had children, Faith didn't understand how devastating Heather's news had been. And if Emily *was* guilty of relying on her daughter too much, Christmas was hardly the time of year to deal with it. But wait a minute. She'd encouraged Heather's independence, hadn't she? After all, the girl was attending school clear across the country. Surely a few days at Christmas wasn't too much to ask.

Emily decided a walk would help her sort through these complicated emotions. She put on her heavy wool coat, laced up her boots and wrapped her hand-knitted red scarf around her neck. She'd knitted an identical scarf for her daughter, although Heather's was purple instead of red, and mailed it off before Thanksgiving. Finally she thrust her hands into warm mittens. It'd snowed overnight and the wind was cold enough to cut to the bone.

The Kennedy kids—ranging from six years old to thirteen—had their sleds out and were racing down the hill in the park. In order of age and size, they scrambled up the steep incline, dragging their sleds behind them. When they reached the top, they all waved excitedly at Emily. Sarah, the youngest, ran over to join her.

"Hello, Mrs. Springer." The youngster smiled up at her with two bottom teeth missing.

"Sarah," Emily said, feigning shock. "Did you lose those two teeth?"

The girl nodded proudly. "My mom pulled them out and I didn't even cry."

"Did the tooth fairy visit?"

"Yes," Sarah told her. "James said there wasn't any such thing, but I put my teeth under my pillow and in the morning there was fifty cents. Mom said if I wanted to believe in the tooth fairy, I could. So I believed and I got two quarters."

"Good for you."

With all the wisdom of her six years, Sarah nodded. "You've got to believe."

"Right," Emily agreed.

"In Santa too!"

As the youngest, Sarah had four older brothers and a sister all too eager to inform her that Santa Claus and his helpers bore a strong resemblance to Mom and Dad.

"Do *you* believe, Mrs. Springer?"

Right now that was a difficult question. Emily was

no longer sure. She wanted to believe in the power of love and family, but her daughter's phone call had forced her to question that. At least a little...

"Do you?" Sarah repeated, staring intently up at Emily.

"Ah..." Then it hit her. She suddenly saw what should've been obvious from the moment she answered the phone that afternoon. "Yes, Sarah," she said, bending down to hug her former kindergarten student.

It was as simple as talking to a child. Sarah understood; sometimes Emily hadn't. *You've got to believe.* There was always a way, and in this instance it was for Emily to book a flight to Boston. If Heather couldn't join her for Christmas, then she'd go to Heather.

The fact that this answer now seemed so effortless unnerved her. The solution had been there from the first, but she'd been so caught up in her sense of loss she'd been blind to it.

Emily had the money for airfare. All she needed was to find a place to stay. Heather would be so surprised, she thought happily. In that instant Emily decided not to tell her, but to make it a genuine surprise—a Christmas gift.

Emily reversed her earlier conviction. What could've been the worst Christmas of her life was destined to be the best!

Chapter Two

Charles Brewster, professor of history at Harvard, pinched the bridge of his nose as he stared at the computer screen. Stretching his neck to see the clock hidden behind two neatly stacked piles of paper, he discovered that it was three o'clock. Charles had to stop and calculate whether that was three in the afternoon or three at night. He often lost track of time, especially since he had an inner office without windows.

And especially since it was December. He hated the whole miserable month—the short days with darkness falling early, the snow, the distractedness of his students and colleagues. *Christmas*. He dreaded it each and every year. Cringed at the very mention of the holidays. Rationally he knew it was because of Monica, who'd chosen Christmas Eve to break off their relationship. She claimed he was distant and inattentive, calling him the perfect example of the absentminded professor. Charles admitted she was probably right, but he'd loved her and been shocked when she'd walked out on him.

Frowning now, Charles realized it was happening already. Christmas was coming, and once again he'd be forced to confront the memories and the bitterness. The truth was, he rarely thought of Monica anymore except at Christmas. He couldn't help it. Boston during December depressed him. In fact, he associated Christmas, especially Christmas in the city, with unhappiness and rejection. It was as if those emotions had detached themselves from Monica and just become part of the season itself.

Standing up, he strolled out of his office and noticed that all the other History Department offices were dark and empty. It must be three at night, then, which meant he hadn't eaten dinner yet. Funny, he distinctly remembered Mrs. Lewis bringing him a tuna sandwich and a cup of hot coffee. His assistant was thoughtful that way. On the other hand, that might've been the day before. Frankly, Charles no longer remembered. His stomach growled, and he rummaged through his desk drawers for a snack. He located a candy bar, eating it hungrily, with only the briefest consideration of how old it might be.

It was too late to head home now, Charles decided. If he left the building, Security would be on him so fast he wouldn't make it to the front door. He'd have to haul out all his identification and explain why he was still here and… No, it was easier just to stay.

He returned his attention to the computer screen and his work. He'd recently been contracted to write a textbook. He'd agreed to a tight deadline because he knew it would help him get through the holidays. Now he wondered if he'd taken on too much.

The next time he glanced up from the computer, Mrs. Lewis had stepped into the office. "Professor Brewster, were you here all night?"

Charles leaned back in his chair and rubbed his hand along his face. "It seems I was."

Shaking her head, she placed a cup of hot, black coffee on his desk.

He sipped it gratefully. "What day is this?" It was a question he asked often—so often that it didn't even cause the department secretary's brow to wrinkle.

"Tuesday, December fourteenth."

"It's the fourteenth already?" He could feel the panic rising.

"Yes, Professor. And you have three student appointments today."

"I see." But all Charles saw was trouble. If his mother wasn't pestering him, then it was his students. He sighed, suddenly exhausted. He'd spent the better part of fifteen hours writing his American history text, focusing on the Colonial era, the Revolutionary War and the country's founding fathers. Much of his work that night had been about the relationship between Thomas Jefferson and Aaron Burr. It wouldn't be light reading, but he knew his history and loved it. If he met his deadline, which Charles was determined to do, and turned in the completed manuscript shortly after the first of the year, it would be published and ready for use by the start of the 2006 autumn classes. High aspirations, but Charles knew he could meet the challenge.

"Your mother just phoned again," Mrs. Lewis informed him. She'd left his office and returned to set the mail on his desk.

Charles sighed. His mother's intentions were good, but she worried about him far too much. For years now, she'd been after him to join her in Arizona for the holidays. Personally, Charles would rather have his fingernails pulled out than spend Christmas with his mother. She suffocated him with her concern and irritated him with her matchmaking efforts. Try as he might, he couldn't make her understand that he wasn't interested in another relationship. His one and only attempt at romance had practically demolished him. After Monica's Christmas Eve defection, he'd shielded himself from further involvement. He was content with his life, although his mother refused to believe it. He didn't *want* a relationship. Women made demands on his time; they were a luxury he couldn't afford if he planned to get ahead in his profession. He wanted to write and teach and there simply weren't enough hours in the day as it was. Frankly that suited him just fine.

If Ray would do him the favor of marrying, Charles would be off the hook. Unfortunately his older brother seemed to be a confirmed bachelor. That left Charles—and his mother wasn't giving up without a fight. At every opportunity she shoved women in his path. Twice in the last six months she'd sent the daughters of friends to Boston to lure him out of his stuffy classroom, as she called it. Both attempts had ended in disaster.

"She wants to know your plans for the holidays."

Charles stiffened. This was how their last conversation had begun. His mother had casually inquired about his plans for Labor Day, and the next thing he knew she'd arranged a dinner engagement for him with one of those young women. That particular one had been a twenty-four-year-old TV production assistant in New York; to say they had nothing in common was putting it mildly. "What did you tell my mother?" he asked.

"That you were occupied and unable to take the call."

From the way Mrs. Lewis's lips thinned, Charles guessed she wasn't pleased at having to engage in this small deception. "Thank you," he muttered.

"She insisted I must know about your plans for Christmas," Mrs. Lewis said in a severe voice.

Apprehension shot up his back. "What did you say?"

Mrs. Lewis crossed her arms and stared down at him. "I said I am not privy to your private arrangements, and that for all I knew you were going out of town."

Actually, that didn't sound like a bad plan. He needed an escape, and the sooner the better. If his mother's behavior was true to pattern, she was about to sic some woman on him. As soon as Mrs. Lewis had made that comment about traveling, the idea took root in his mind. It would do him good to get out of the city. He didn't care where he went as long as it was away from Boston, away from his seasonal misery. Someplace quiet would suit him nicely. Someplace where he could work and not worry about what time or day it happened to be.

"Hmm. That has possibilities," he murmured thoughtfully.

The older woman didn't seem to know what he was talking about. His students often wore the same confused look, as if he were speaking in a foreign language.

"Traveling." The decision made now, he stood and reached for his overcoat. "Yes."

Her gaze narrowed. "Excuse me?"

"That was an excellent idea. I'm leaving town for the holidays." All he wanted was peace and quiet; that should be simple enough to arrange.

"Where?" Mrs. Lewis stammered, following him out of his office.

He shrugged. "I really don't care."

"Well, I could call a travel agent for recommendations."

"Don't bother."

A travel agent might book him into some area where he'd be surrounded by people and festivities centered on the Christmas holidays. Any contact with others was out of the question. He wanted to find a place where he'd be completely alone, with no chance of being disturbed. And if possible, he wanted to find a place where Christmas wasn't a big deal.

He told Mrs. Lewis all this, then asked her for suggestions. He turned down Vermont, Aspen, Santa Fe and Disney World.

Disney World!

At her despairing look, he sighed again. "Never mind," he said. "I'll do it myself."

She nodded and seemed relieved.

Later that day, Charles had to admit that finding an obscure location for travel on such short notice was difficult. Taking his briefcase with him, he walked to his condo, not far from the university area. But after he'd showered, heated up a microwave lasagna for his dinner and slept, he tackled the project with renewed enthusiasm. It was now shortly after 8:00 p.m.

After calling half a dozen airlines, he realized he was seeking the impossible. Not a man to accept defeat, Charles went online to do his own investigative work. It was while he was surfing the Internet that he found a site on which people traded homes for short periods.

One such notice was from a woman who'd posted a message: **Desperately Seeking Home in Boston for Christmas Holidays.**

Charles read the message twice, awed by his good fortune. This woman, a schoolteacher in a small town in Washington State, sought a residence in Boston for two weeks over the Christmas holidays. She could travel after December 17th and return as late as December 31st.

The dates were perfect for Charles. He started to get excited. This might actually work without costing him an arm and a leg. Since he didn't have to register in a hotel, his mother would have no obvious means of tracking him. Oh, this was very good news indeed.

Charles answered the woman right away.

From: "Charles Brewster" <hadisbad@charternet.net>
To: "Emily Springer" springere@aal.com
Sent: December 14, 2004
Subject: Trading Places
Dear Ms. Springer,
I'm responding to the DESPERATELY SEEKING IN BOSTON advertisement shown on the Trading Homes Web site. I live in Boston and teach at Harvard. My condo is a two-bedroom, complete with all modern conveniences. You can e-mail me with your questions at the address listed above. I eagerly await your reply.
Sincerely,
Charles Brewster

Before long Charles received a response. Naturally, she had a number of questions. He had a few of his own, but once he was assured that he'd be completely alone in a small Eastern Washington town, Charles agreed to the swap. He supplied references, and she offered her own.

A flurry of e-mails quickly passed between them as they figured out the necessary details. Emily seemed to think she owed him an explanation as to why she was interested in Boston. He didn't tell her that he didn't care about her reasons.

He certainly didn't mention his own. He rather enjoyed the notion of spending time in a town called Leavenworth. If he remembered correctly, a big federal prison was situated in the area. As far as Charles was concerned, that was even better. The less celebrating going on, the happier he'd be. He could spend the holidays in a nice, quiet prison town without any Christmas fuss.

His remaining concern was buying a plane ticket, but once again the online travel sites came to his rescue. Charles had no objection to flying a red-eye, since half the time he didn't know whether it was day or night.

"Everything's been arranged," he announced to Mrs. Lewis the following morning.

She responded with a brief nod. "So you have decided to travel."

"I have."

She held up her hand. "Don't tell me any of the details."

He stared at her. "Why not?"

"In case your mother asks, I can honestly tell her I don't know."

"Excellent idea." He beamed at the brilliance of her suggestion. For once, he was going to outsmart his dear, sweet matchmaker of a mother and at the same time blot Christmas from the calendar. School was closing for winter recess and if she couldn't reach him, she'd assume he wasn't answering his phone, which he rarely did, anyway—even before caller ID. And suppose his mother found some way to get hold of Mrs. Lewis during the Christmas holidays? It wouldn't matter, because Mrs. Lewis didn't know a thing! This was more satisfactory by the minute.

For two blessed weeks in December, he was going to escape Christmas and his mother in one fell swoop.

No question about it, life didn't get any better than this.

Chapter Three

The bell rang, dismissing Faith Kerrigan's last junior-high literature class of the afternoon. Her students were out of the room so fast, anyone might think the building was in danger of exploding. She could understand their eagerness to leave. When classes were dismissed for winter break at the end of the week, she'd be ready—more than ready.

"Faith?" Sharon Carson stuck her head in the doorway. "You want to hit the mall this afternoon?"

Faith cringed. The crowds were going to be horrendous, and it would take a braver woman than she to venture into a mall this close to the holidays. One advantage of being single was that Faith didn't have a lot of Christmas shopping to do. That thought, however, depressed her.

She was an aunt three times over, thanks to her younger sister. Faith loved her nephews, but she'd always dreamed of being a mother herself one day. She'd said goodbye to that dream when she divorced. At the time she hadn't realized it; she'd blithely assumed she'd remarry, but to this point she hadn't met anyone who even remotely interested her. She hadn't guessed it would be that difficult to meet a decent man, but apparently she'd been wrong. Now thirty, she'd begun to feel her chances were growing bleaker by the day.

"Not tonight, Sharon, but thanks."

Her fellow teacher and friend leaned against the door of her classroom. "You're usually up for a trip to the mall. Is something bothering you?"

"Not really." Other than the sorry state of her love life, the only thing on Faith's mind was getting through the next few days of classes.

"Are you sure?" Sharon pressed.

"I'm sure." Faith glanced over at her and smiled. She was tall, the same height as Faith at five foot eight, and ten years older. Odd that her two best friends were forty. Both Emily and Sharon were slightly overweight, while Faith kept her figure trim and athletic. Emily was an undiscovered beauty. She was also the perfect kindergarten teacher, patient and gentle. She looked far younger than her years, with short curly brown hair and dark eyes. Unlike Faith, she wasn't interested in sports. Emily felt she got enough physical exercise racing after five-year-olds all day and had no interest in joining the gym or owning a treadmill. Come to think of it, Faith wasn't sure Leavenworth even had a gym.

Faith ran five miles three times a week and did a seven-mile-run each weekend. She left the races to those who enjoyed collecting T-shirts. She wasn't one of them. The running habit had started shortly after her separation, and she'd never stopped.

"You haven't mentioned Emily lately. What's up with her?" Sharon asked and came all the way into the room. The summer before, when Sharon and her family had taken a trip north to Washington State, Faith had suggested they visit Leavenworth. As soon as Emily learned Faith's friend would be in the area, she'd insisted on showing them the town. Emily was the consummate host and a fabulous cook. Sharon had come back full of tales about Leavenworth and Emily.

"I talked to her on Sunday." Faith began erasing the blackboard, but paused in the middle of a sweeping motion. "Funny you should mention her, because she's been on my mind ever since."

"I thought you two e-mailed back and forth every day."

"We do—well, almost every day." Faith had sent Emily an e-mail the day before and hadn't heard back, which told her Emily was especially busy. No doubt there'd be a message waiting for her once she got home.

She turned to face Sharon. "I think I might've offended her." Now that she thought about it, Faith realized she probably had. "Emily phoned, which she rarely does, to tell me Heather won't be coming home for Christmas. I told Emily it was time Heather had her own life and to make the best of it." Given the opportunity, she'd gladly take back those words. "I can't believe I wasn't more sympathetic," Faith said, pulling out the desk chair to sit down. She felt dreadful. Her friend had phoned looking for understanding, and Faith had let her down.

"Don't be so hard on yourself," Sharon said. She slipped into one of the student desks.

"Emily doesn't want to be alone over Christmas, and who can blame her?"

"No one wants to be alone at Christmas."

Faith didn't; in fact she'd made plans to visit Penny and join in the festivities with her nephews. "I was completely and utterly insensitive. Poor Emily." No wonder she hadn't answered Faith's e-mail.

"What are you going to do?" Sharon asked.

"What makes you think I'm going to do anything?"

A smile crept over Sharon's face. "Because I know you. I can tell from the look in your eyes."

"Well, you're right. I have an idea."

"What?"

Faith was almost beside herself with glee. "I'm going to surprise Emily and visit her for Christmas."

"I thought you were spending the holidays with your sister."

"I was, but Penny will understand." The truth, Faith realized, was that Penny might even be grateful.

"It's pretty hard to book a flight at this late date," Sharon said, frowning.

"I know…. I haven't figured that out yet." Booking a flight could be a problem, but Faith was convinced she'd find a way, even if it meant flying in the dead of night. There had to be a flight into the Seattle-Tacoma airport at some point between Friday night and Christmas Day.

"My sister-in-law works for a travel agent. Would you like her number?"

"Thanks, Sharon."

They walked to the faculty lounge together and got their purses out of their lockers. Sharon pulled out her cell phone, then scrolled down until she found the number. Faith quickly made a note of it.

"If there's a flight to be had, Carrie will find it," Sharon assured her.

"Thanks again."

"Are you going to call Emily and let her know your plans?" Sharon asked as they left the school building, walking toward the parking lot.

"Not yet. I don't want to get her hopes up if this turns out to be impossible."

"If worse comes to worst, I suppose you could always drive."

"I don't think so." Faith had done it often enough to realize she didn't want to take the Interstate in the middle of winter. The pass over the Siskiyous could be hellish this time of year. It wasn't a trip she wanted to make on her own, either.

"Don't worry—Carrie will get you a flight," Sharon said confidently.

As soon as she was in her car, Faith pulled out her own cell phone and dialed the travel agency. Carrie was extremely helpful and promised to get back to her as soon as she could.

Now that she had a plan, Faith was starting to feel excited. She called her sister soon after she arrived home, and the instant Penny picked up the phone, Faith could hear her three nephews fighting in the background. It sounded as if they were close to killing one another by the time the conversation ended.

Penny had made a token display of disappointment, but Faith didn't think her sister was too distressed. And Faith had to admit she was looking forward to a different kind of holiday herself. One without bickering kids—much as she loved them—and the same old routines. Still, her family was important to her, and she'd promised to visit right after New Year's.

Because she had someplace to go and family to be with, Faith hadn't really listened to what Emily had tried to tell her, hadn't really understood. Emily adored her daughter, of course, but Heather's absence was only part of the problem. What bothered her just as much was the prospect of spending perhaps the most significant holiday of the year by herself. In retrospect, Faith was astonished she hadn't recognized that earlier. She was a better friend than this and she was about to prove it.

After Faith had finished talking to her sister, she immediately sat down at her computer and logged on to the Internet. To her surprise Emily hadn't left her a message. Undeterred, she sent one off.

From: "Faith"<fkerriganinca@network.com>
To: "Emily"<springere@aal.com>
Sent: Thursday, December 16, 2004
Subject: Gift to arrive

Dear Emily,
I haven't heard from you all week. Forgive me for not being more of a friend.
Look for a present to arrive shortly.
Get back to me soon.
Love,
Faith

Half an hour later, the travel agent phoned. "I've got good news and bad news."

"Did you get me a flight?"

"Yes, that worked out fine. I got you into Seattle, but all the flights into Wenatchee are full. That's the bad news." Leavenworth was a few hours outside Seattle, but Faith could manage that easily enough with a rental car.

"I'll book a car," she said.

"I thought of that, too," Carrie went on to explain, "but this is a busy time of year for car rental agencies. The only vehicle available in all of Seattle is a seven-person van."

"Oh." Faith bit her lower lip.

"I reserved it because it was the last car left, but I can cancel the reservation if you don't want it."

Faith didn't take more than a few seconds to decide. "No, I'll take it."

On December twenty-fifth, she intended to be with Emily in Leavenworth. Not only that, she intended to bring Christmas with her—lock, stock and decorations.

Have Yule, will travel.

Chapter Four

In Emily's opinion, everything had worked out perfectly—other than the fact that she hadn't been able to reach Heather to let her know she was arriving. Not that it mattered. Heather would be as thrilled as she was. When Christmas came, the two of them would be together.

Early Sunday morning, Emily caught the short commuter flight out of Wenatchee and landed thirty minutes later at Sea-Tac Airport. Within an hour, Emily was on a nonstop flight from Seattle to Boston.

A mere seven days following her conversation with Heather, Emily was on her way across the entire United States to spend Christmas with her daughter. At the same time Charles Brewster, who sounded like a stereotypical absentminded history professor, was on his way to Leavenworth. Apparently their paths would cross somewhere over the middle of the country, her plane headed east and his headed west.

Emily would spend two glorious weeks with Heather, and Charles would have two weeks to explore Washington State—or do whatever he wanted. They were due to trade back on January first.

Two glorious weeks in Boston. Emily realized Heather had to work on papers and study, but she didn't mind. At least they'd be able to enjoy Christmas Day together and that was what mattered most.

The one negative was that Emily didn't know her daughter's schedule. Emily had repeatedly attempted to contact her, but Heather hadn't returned her messages. Tracy, Heather's roommate, hadn't said anything outright, but Emily had the feeling Heather didn't spend much time in her dorm room. She was obviously working longer hours than she'd let on. Actually, surprising her would be a good thing, Emily thought as she called Heather from Charles Brewster's condo. It would force her to take some time off and—

Surprise her she did.

"Mother," Heather cried into the receiver loudly enough to hurt Emily's eardrum. "You *can't* be in Boston."

Emily realized her arrival was a shock, but Heather seemed more dismayed than pleased.

"I didn't know you had a cell phone," Emily said. It would've saved them both a great deal of frustration had she been able to reach Heather earlier. She'd called the dorm room as soon as she'd landed and Tracy had given Emily a cell number.

"The phone isn't mine," Heather protested. "It belongs to a...friend."

"Ben?"

"No," she said. "Ben is old news."

Information she hadn't bothered to share with her mother, Emily mused. "Where are you?"

"That's not important." Heather sounded almost angry. "Where are *you*?"

Emily rattled off the address, but it didn't sound as if Heather had written anything down. Charles Brewster's condo had proved to be something of a disappointment—not that she was complaining. She'd found it easily enough and settled into the guest room, but it was modern and sterile, devoid of personality or any sign of Christmas.

"I'm so eager to see you," Emily told her daughter. She'd been in town for several hours and they still hadn't connected. "Why don't you come here, where I'm staying and—"

"I'd rather we met at the Starbucks across the street from my dormitory."

"But…" Emily couldn't understand why her daughter wouldn't want to come to her. Her attitude was puzzling, to say the least.

"Mother." Heather paused. "It would be better if we met at Starbucks."

"All right."

"Are you far from there?"

Emily didn't know her way around Boston, but the Harvard campus was within walking distance of the condo. Emily figured she'd find the coffee place without too much trouble, and she told Heather that.

"Meet me there in an hour," Heather snapped.

"Of course, but—"

The line went dead and Emily stared at the receiver, shocked that her own daughter had hung up on her. Or maybe the phone had gone dead. Maybe the battery had run out….

With a little while before she had to leave, Emily walked around the condominium with all its modern conveniences. The kitchen was equipped with stainless steel appliances and from the look of it, Emily doubted anyone had so much as turned on a burner. The refrigerator still had the owner's manual in the bottom drawer and almost nothing else. As soon as she could manage it, Emily would find a grocery store.

Everything about the condo was spotless—and barren. Barren was a good word, she decided. Charles Brewster apparently didn't spend much time in his luxurious home. In her opinion his taste in furniture left something to be desired, too. All the pieces were modern, oddly shaped and in her opinion, uncomfortable. She suspected he'd given a designer free rein and then found the look so discordant that he left home whenever possible.

There wasn't a single Christmas decoration. Thank goodness Emily had brought a bit of Christmas cheer with her. The first thing she unpacked was their hand-knit Christmas stockings.

Emily's mother, who'd died a couple of years before Peter, had knit her stocking when Emily was five years old, and she'd knit Heather's too. It just wouldn't be Christmas without their stockings. She hung them from the mantel, using a couple of paper-weights she found in the study to secure them. The angel was carefully packaged in a carry-on. She unwrapped that and set it on the mantel, too. Then she arranged a few other favorite pieces—a tiny sled with a little girl atop, a Santa Heather had bought with her own money when she was ten, a miniature gift, gaily wrapped.

Her suitcases were empty now, but several Christmas decorations remained to be placed about the condo. Emily thought she'd save those until later, when Heather could take part. That way it'd be just like home.

Assuming it would take her no more than thirty minutes to walk to Starbucks, Emily put on her coat, then stepped out of the condo, took the elevator to the marble foyer and hurried onto the sidewalk. Although it was only mid-afternoon, it resembled dusk. Dark ominous clouds hung overhead and the threat of snow was unmistakable.

Perhaps Heather would suggest a walk across the campus in the falling snow. They could pretend they were back home.

Emily arrived at Starbucks in fifteen minutes and bought a cup of coffee. While she waited for her daughter, she sat at the table next to the window and watched the young people stroll past. Although classes had officially been dismissed for winter break, plenty of students were still in evidence.

A large motorcycle roared past, and Emily winced at the loud, discordant sound. She sipped her coffee, watching the Harley—she assumed it was a Harley because that was the only brand she'd ever heard of. The motorcycle made a U-turn in the middle of the street and pulled into an empty parking space outside the coffee shop. Actually, it wasn't a real space, more of a gap between two parked cars.

The rider turned off the engine, climbed off the bike and removed his black bubble-like helmet. He was an unpleasant-looking fellow, Emily thought. His hair was long and tied at the base of his neck in a ponytail, which he'd flipped over his shoulder. He was dressed completely in black leather, much of his face covered with a thick beard.

A second rider, also dressed in black leather, slipped off the bike and removed a helmet. Emily blinked, certain she must be seeing things. If she didn't know better, she'd think the second person was her own daughter. But that wasn't possible. Was it?

Heather's twin placed her hand on the man's forearm, said something Emily couldn't hear and then headed into Starbucks alone. The Harley man stayed outside, guarding his bike.

Once the door opened and the girl walked inside, it was all too obvious that she was indeed Heather.

Aghast, Emily stood, nearly tipping over her coffee. *"Heather?"*

"Why didn't you let me know you were coming?" her daughter demanded.

"It's good to see you, too," Emily mumbled sarcastically.

Heather's eyes narrowed. "Frankly, Mother, it's *not* good to see you."

Emily swallowed a gasp. In her wildest imaginings,

she'd never dreamed her daughter would say such a thing to her. Without being aware of it, Emily sank back into her chair.

Heather pulled out the chair across from her and sat down.

"Who's your...friend?" Emily asked, nodding toward the window.

"That's Elijah," Heather responded, defiance in every word.

"He doesn't have a last name?"

"No, just Elijah."

Emily sighed. "I see."

"I don't think you do," Heather said pointedly. "You should've told me you were coming to Boston."

"I tried," Emily burst out. "I talked to Tracy five times and left that many messages. Tracy said she'd let you know I'd phoned."

"She did...."

"Then why didn't you return my calls?"

Heather dropped her gaze. "Because I was afraid you were going to send me on a guilt trip and I didn't want to deal with it."

"Send you on a *guilt* trip?"

"You do that, you know? Make me feel guilty."

Despite her irritation, Emily did her best to remain calm. Now she understood why her daughter had insisted they meet at the coffee shop. She didn't want

Emily to make a scene, which she admitted she was close to doing.

"I left *five* messages," Emily reminded her.

"I know—but I've been staying with friends and didn't realize you'd phoned until Tracy got in touch with me."

Staying with friends? Yeah, right. Emily's gaze flew out the window. Her daughter and that…that Neanderthal?

"I love him," Heather said boldly.

Emily managed to stay seated. "If that's the case, why don't you bring him inside so we can meet?"

"Because…" Heather hesitated and then squared her shoulders as if gathering her courage. "I didn't want him to hear what you're planning to say."

"About what?" This made no sense whatsoever.

"None of that matters. I'm leaving town with Elijah. In other words, I won't be in Boston over the holidays."

Emily shook her head slightly, wondering if she'd heard correctly. "I beg your pardon?"

"Elijah and I and a couple of other friends are riding down to Florida."

"For Christmas?" Emily *knew* something was wrong with her hearing now. There simply had to be. "On motorcycles?"

"Yes, for Christmas. And yes, on motorcycles. We're sick of this weather and want to spend our holiday on the beach."

Emily was completely speechless.

"You don't have anything to say?" Heather asked angrily. "I figured you'd have lots of opinions to share."

Emily's mouth opened and closed twice while she gathered her thoughts. "I traded homes with a stranger, traveled across the country and now you're telling me you won't be here for Christmas?" Her voice rose on the last word.

Heather's eyes flashed. "That's exactly what I'm saying. I'm of age and I make my own decisions."

Emily's jaw sagged in dismay. "You mean you're actually going to abandon me here—"

"You didn't bother to check your plans with me before you boarded that plane, did you, Mother? That's unfortunate because I've made other arrangements for Christmas. As far as I'm concerned, this problem is all yours."

"You said you had to work." That clearly had been a blatant lie.

"There you go," Heather cried. "You're trying to make me feel guilty."

"If you'd been honest—"

"You don't want me to be honest!" Heather challenged.

The truth of it was, she was right. Emily would rather not know that her daughter was associating with a member of some motorcycle gang.

"Go then," Emily said, waving her hand toward the door. "Have a wonderful time."

Heather leaped out of the chair as if she couldn't get away fast enough. "You can't blame me for this!"

"I'm not blaming you for anything," she said tiredly. Heaven forbid her daughter should accuse her of throwing guilt.

"This is all your own doing."

Emily stared silently into the distance.

"Nothing you say is going to make me change my mind," Heather insisted, as if wanting her to argue.

Emily didn't imagine it would. She felt physically ill, but she held onto her dignity. Pride demanded that she not let her daughter know how badly she'd hurt her.

Rushing out the door, Heather grabbed the black helmet, placed it on her head and climbed onto the back of the motorcycle. Elijah with no last name was already on the bike and within seconds they disappeared down the street.

Emily's opinion of this coming Christmas did an about-face.

This was destined to be the worst one of her life. Not only was she alone, but she was in a strange town, without a single friend. And her daughter had just broken her heart.

Chapter Five

"For heaven's sake, what is this?" Charles stood outside the gingerbread house in the middle of Santa's village feeling total dismay. There had to be some mistake—some vast, terrible mistake. Nothing else would explain the fact that after flying three thousand miles, he'd landed smack-dab in the middle of Christmas Town, complete with ice-skating rink, glittering lights and Christmas music.

He closed his eyes, hoping, praying, this nightmare would vanish and he could settle down in a nice quiet prison community. When he opened them, it was even worse than Charles had imagined. A little kid was staring up at him.

"I'm Sarah," she announced.

He said nothing.

"I lost two teeth." She proceeded to pull down her lower lip in order to reveal the empty spaces in her mouth.

"Is this where Emily Springer lives?" Charles asked, nodding toward the bungalow. He was uncomfortable around children, mainly because he didn't know any.

"She went to Boston to spend Christmas with her daughter," Sarah informed him.

"I know." So he was in the right town. Damn.

"She keeps the key under the flower pot if you need to get inside."

Charles cocked his eyebrows. "She told you that?"

"Everyone in town knows where the key is." As if to prove it, Sarah walked over to the porch, lifted up the pot and produced the key, which she proudly displayed.

A one-horse open sleigh drove past, bells ringing, resembling something straight off a Christmas card. It didn't get any more grotesque than this. Ice skaters circled the rink in the park directly across the street from him. They were dressed in period costumes and singing in three-part harmony.

Rolling his suitcase behind him and clutching his laptop, Charles approached the house. It reminded him of an illustration, too cozy and perfect to be true, with its scalloped edging and colorful shutters. The porch had a swing and a rocking chair. Had he been Norman Rockwell, he would have found a canvas and painted it. Charles sighed heavily. This must be his punishment for trying to avoid Christmas.

"My mom's bringing you cookies," Sarah told him as she followed him up the steps.

"Tell her not to bother."

"She does it to be neighborly."

"I don't want neighbors."

"You don't?"

The little girl looked crushed.

He didn't mean to hurt the kid's feelings, but he wasn't interested in joining a Christmas commune. He simply wasn't socially inclined. All he wanted was to be left alone so he could write—and ignore anything to do with Christmas. Clearly, he'd been mistaken about this town—where was the prison? Keeping to his all-work-and-no-Yule agenda was going to be more of a challenge than he'd planned.

"Thank your mother for me, but explain that I came here to work," he told the little girl, making an effort to mollify her with politeness.

"But it's *Christmas*."

"I'm well aware of the season," he said, stabbing the key into the lock. "Let your mother know I prefer not to be disturbed." He hoped the kid would take the hint, too.

Sarah jutted out her lower lip. "Okay."

Good, she got the message. Charles opened the front door and stepped inside. He should've been prepared.... If Leavenworth was Santa's village, then stepping into this house was like walking into a fairy tale. The furniture was large and old-fashioned and bulky, with lots of lace and doilies. He'd traded homes with Goldilocks. Well, with the Three Bears, anyway. A grandfather clock chimed in the living room and logs were arranged in the fireplace, ready for a match. A knitted afghan was draped across the back of the overstuffed sofa. A green and blue braided rug covered the hardwood floor.

"Oh, brother," Charles sighed, truly discouraged. He abandoned his suitcase and laptop in the entry and walked into the kitchen. Emily had left him a note propped against the holly wreath that served as a centerpiece on the round oak table. Charles was almost afraid to read it.

After a moment he reached for it, read it, then tossed it in the garbage. She'd left him dinner in the refrigerator. All he had to do was heat it in the microwave.

Dinner. Cookies from the neighbor. "Jingle Bells" in a one-horse open sleigh gliding back and forth in front of the house. If *that* wasn't bad enough, the entire street, indeed the whole town, glittered with Christmas lights that blinked from every conceivable corner. This was madness. Sheer madness. He hadn't escaped Christmas; he'd dived headfirst into the middle of it.

The first thing Charles did before he unpacked was pull down every shade on every window he could find. That, at least, blocked out the lights. He found an empty bedroom, set his suitcase on a chair and took out the work materials he needed.

The doorbell chimed and he groaned inwardly, bracing himself for another confrontation with the Christmas kid. Or her mother, bearing gifts of cookies.

It wasn't a woman with a plate of cookies or the child who'd accosted him earlier. Instead there were *six* of them, six children who stared up at him in wide-eyed wonder. They were dressed in winter gear from head to toe, with only their eyes and noses visible behind thick wool scarves and hand-knit hats. Their noses were bright red and their eyes watery. Melting snow dripped puddles onto the porch.

"Do you want to come outside? Go sledding with us?" the oldest of the group asked, his scarf moving where his mouth must be.

"No." Charles couldn't think of anything more to add.

"We have an extra sled you can use."

"I—no, thanks."

"Okay," the second-tallest boy answered.

No one budged.

"You sure?" the first boy asked.

Someone shouted from nearby. An adult voice from what he could tell.

"That's our mom," one of the children said. The little girl from before.

"We were supposed to leave you alone," another girl told him. At least he thought it was a girl.

"You should listen to your mother."

"Do you?"

The kid had him there. "Not always."

"Us neither." The boy's eyes smiled at him and Charles realized he'd made a friend, which was unfortunate.

"Emily said you were a teacher, too."

"I'm writing a book and I won't have time to play in the snow." He started to close the door.

"Not at all?" The oldest boy asked the question with a complete sense of horror.

"It's Christmas," another reminded him.

The woman's voice sounded again, shriller this time.

"We got to go."

"Bye," Charles said and, despite himself, found that he was grinning when he closed the door. His amusement died a quick death once he was back inside the house. Despite his attempt to block out all evidence of Christmas, he was well aware that it waited right outside, ready to pounce on him the minute he peeked out.

Grumbling under his breath, he returned to the kitchen and grudgingly set his dinner in the microwave. Some kind of casserole, duly labeled "Charles." He resisted the urge to call Emily Springer and tell her exactly what he thought of her little Christmas deception. He would, too, if she'd misled him—only she hadn't. He blamed himself for this. Because he'd just realized something—he'd confused Leavenworth, Washington, with Leavenworth, Kansas.

The doorbell chimed once more, and Charles looked at the ceiling, rolling his eyes and groaning audibly. Apparently he was going to have to be more forthright with the family next door. He stomped across the room and hauled open the front door. He wanted to make it clear that he didn't appreciate the disturbances.

No one was there.

He stuck his head out the door and glanced in both directions.

No one.

Then he noticed a plate of decorated cookies sitting on the porch. They were wrapped in red cellophane, which was tied with a silver bow. His first instinct was to pretend he hadn't seen them. At the last second, he reached down, grabbed the plate and slammed the door shut. He turned the lock, and leaned against the wall, breathing fast.

He was in the wrong Leavenworth, but he might as well be in prison, since he wouldn't be able to leave the house, or even open the door, for fear of being ambushed by Christmas carolers, cookies and children.

Not exactly what he'd had in mind...

Chapter Six

Bernice Brewster was beside herself with frustration. For two days she'd tried to reach her son Charles, to no avail. He refused to use a cell phone and the one she'd purchased for him sat in a drawer somewhere. She was sure he'd never even charged the battery.

Growing up in Boston, Charles had been fascinated by history, particularly the original Thirteen Colonies. Now look at him! Granted, that interest had taken him far; unfortunately it seemed to be his *only* interest. If he wasn't standing in front of a classroom full of students—hanging on his every word as she fondly imagined—then he was buried in a book. Now, it appeared, he was writing his very own.

Why, oh why, couldn't her sons be like her friends' children, who were constantly causing them heart-ache and worry? Instead, she'd borne two sons who had to be the most loving, kindest sons on God's green earth, but... The problem was that they didn't understand one of the primary duties of a son—to provide his parents with grandchildren.

Bernice couldn't understand where she'd gone wrong. If there was anything to be grateful for, it was that Bernard hadn't lived long enough to discover what a disappointment their two sons had turned out to be in the family department.

Charles was the younger of the two. Rayburn, eight years his senior, lived in New York City and worked for one of the big publishers there. He insisted on being called Ray, although she never thought of him as anything but Rayburn. He was a gifted man who'd risen quickly in publishing, although he changed houses or companies so often she couldn't hope to keep track of where he was or exactly what he did. At last mention, he'd said something about the name of the publisher changing because his company had merged with another. The merger had apparently netted him a promotion.

Like his younger brother, however, Rayburn was a disappointment in the area of marriage. Her oldest son was married to his job. He was in his mid-forties now and she'd given up hope that he'd ever settle down with a wife and family. Rayburn lived and breathed publishing.

Charles, it seemed, was her only chance for grandchildren, slight though that chance might be. He was such a nice young man and for a while, years ago now, there'd been such promise when he'd fallen head over heels in love. Monica. Oh, yes, she remembered Monica, a conniving shallow little bitch who'd broken her son's heart. On Christmas Eve, yet.

What was wrong with all those women in Boston and New York? Both her sons were attractive; Rayburn and Charles possessed their father's striking good looks, not that either had ever taken advantage of that. Bernice suspected Rayburn had been involved with various women, but obviously there'd never been anyone special.

Sitting in her favorite chair with the phone beside her, Bernice wondered what to do next. This was a sorry, sorry state of affairs. While her friends in the Arizona retirement community brought out book after book filled with darling pictures of their grandchildren, she had nothing to show except photos of her Pomeranian, FiFi. There were only so many pictures of the dog she could pass around. Even she was tired of looking at photographs of FiFi.

Bernice petted the small dog and with a brooding

sense that something was terribly wrong, reached for the phone. She pushed speed dial for Charles's number and closed her eyes with impatience, waiting for the call to connect.

After one short ring, someone answered. "Hello."

Bernice gasped. The voice was soft and distinctly female. She couldn't believe her ears.

"Hello?"

"Is this the residence of Charles Brewster?" Bernice asked primly. "Professor Charles Brewster?"

"Yes, it is."

Of course it was Charles's condominium. The number was programmed into her phone and Bernice trusted technology. Shocked, she slammed down the receiver and stared, horrified, at the golf course outside.

Charles had a woman at his place. A woman he hadn't mentioned to his own mother, which could mean only one thing. Her son didn't want her to know anything about this...this female. All kinds of frightening scenarios flew into her mind. Charles consorting with a gold digger—or worse. Charles held hostage. Charles... She shook her head. No, she had to take control here.

Still in shock, Bernice picked up the phone again and pushed the top speed-dial button, which would connect her with Rayburn's New York apartment. He was often more difficult to reach than Charles. Luck was with her, however, and Rayburn answered after the third ring.

"Rayburn," Bernice cried in near-panic, not giving him a chance to greet her.

"Mother, what's wrong?"

"When was the last time you spoke with your brother?" she demanded breathlessly.

Rayburn seemed to need time to think about this, but Bernice was in no condition to wait. "Something is wrong with Charles! I'm so worried."

"Why don't you start at the beginning?"

"I *am*," she cried.

"Now, Mother…"

"Hear me out before you *Now, Mother* me." The more she thought about a strange woman answering Charles's phone, the more alarmed she became. Ever since that dreadful Monica had broken off the relationship… Ever since her, he'd gone out of his way to avoid women. In fact, he seemed oblivious to them and rejected every attempt she'd made to match him up.

"Your brother has a woman living with him," she said, her voice trembling.

Silence followed her announcement. "Mother, have you been drinking hot buttered rum again?"

"No," she snapped, insulted he'd ask such a thing.

"Hear me out. I haven't been able to get hold of Charles for two days. I left messages on his answering machine, and he never returned a single call."

Her son was listening, and for that Bernice was grateful.

"Go on," he said without inflection.

"Just now, not more than five minutes ago, I called Charles again. A woman answered the phone." She squeezed her eyes closed. "She had a...sexy voice."

"Perhaps it was a cleaning woman."

"On a Monday?"

"Maybe it was a colleague. A friend from the History Department."

Bernice maintained a stubborn silence.

"You're sure about this?" Rayburn finally said.

"As sure as I live and breathe. Your brother has a woman in his home—living there."

"Just because she answered the phone doesn't mean she's living with Charles."

"You and I both know your brother would never allow just anyone to answer the phone."

Rayburn seemed to agree; a casual visitor wouldn't be answering his brother's phone.

"Good for him," Rayburn said with what sounded like a chuckle.

"How can you say that?" Bernice cried. "It's obvious that this woman must be completely unacceptable."

"Now, Mother..."

"Why wouldn't Charles tell us about her?"

"I don't know, but I think you're jumping to conclusions."

"I'm not! I just *know* something's wrong. Perhaps she tricked her way into his home, killed him and—"

"You've been watching too many crime shows," Rayburn chastised.

"Perhaps I have, but I won't rest until I get to the bottom of this."

"Fine." Her oldest son apparently grasped how serious she was, because he asked, "What do you want me to do?"

"Oh, Rayburn," she said with a sob, dabbing her nose with a delicate hankie. "I don't know how I'd manage without my sons to look out for me."

"Mother..."

"Take the train to Boston and investigate this situation. Report back to me ASAP."

"I can phone him and handle this in five minutes."

"No." She was insistent. "I want you to check it out with your own eyes. God only knows what your brother's gotten himself into with this woman. I just know whoever it is must be taking advantage of Charles."

"*Mother*. This is Christmas week and—"

"I know what time of year it is, Rayburn, and I realize you have a life of your own. A life that's much too busy to include your mother. But I'll tell you right now that I won't sleep a wink until I hear what's happened to Charles."

There was a pause.

"All right," Rayburn muttered. "I'll take the train to Boston and check up on Charles."

"Thank God." She could breathe easier now.

Chapter Seven

The Boeing 767 bounced against the tarmac and jarred Faith Kerrigan awake. She bolted upright and realized that she'd just landed in Seattle. She glanced at her watch; it was just after seven. She'd had less than four hours sleep the entire night.

She'd survive. Any discomfort would be well worth the look of joy and surprise on Emily's face when Faith arrived and announced she'd be joining her friend for Christmas.

Remembering that was a better wake-up than a triple-shot espresso. Although the flight—which was completely full—had left the Bay area at 5:00 a.m., Faith had been up since two. Her lone suitcase was packed to the bursting point and she'd stuffed her carry-on until the zipper threatened to pop. After filing off the plane and collecting her suitcase, she dragged everything to the car rental agency. Thankfully, an attendant was available despite the early hour.

Faith stepped up to the counter and managed a smile. "Hi."

"Happy holidays," the young woman greeted her. The name tag pinned to her blouse identified her as Theresa.

With her confirmation number in hand, Faith leaned against the counter and asked, "Will you need my credit card?" She couldn't remember if she'd given the number to her travel agent earlier.

Theresa nodded and slid over a sheaf of papers to fill out. Faith dug in the bottom of her purse for her favorite pen.

The girl on the other side of the counter reminded her of Heather, and she wondered briefly if Theresa was a college student deprived of spending Christmas with her family because of her job.

The phone pealed; Theresa answered immediately. After announcing the name of the agency, followed by "Theresa speaking," she went silent. Her eyes widened as she listened to whoever was on the other end. Then, for some inexplicable reason, the young woman's gaze landed on her.

"That's terrible," Theresa murmured, steadily eyeing Faith.

Faith shifted her feet uncomfortably and waited.

"No...she's here now. I don't know what to tell you. Sure, I can ask, but...yes. Okay. Let me put you on hold."

Faith shifted her weight to the other foot. This sounded ominous.

Theresa held the telephone receiver against her shoulder. "There's been a problem," she said. Her dark eyes held a pleading look.

"What kind of problem?"

The young woman sighed. "Earlier we rented a van exactly like yours to a group of actors and, unfortunately, theirs broke down. Even more unfortunate, we don't have a replacement we can give them. On top of that, it doesn't look like the van they were driving can be easily fixed."

Faith could tell what was coming next. "You want me to give up the van I reserved."

"The thing is, we don't have a single car on the lot to give you in exchange."

Faith would've liked to help, but she had no other means of getting to Leavenworth. "The only reason I reserved the van is because it was the last car available."

"My manager is well aware of that."

"Where is this group headed?" All she needed the

van for was to get to Leavenworth. Once Faith reached her destination, she'd be with Emily, who had her own vehicle. She explained that.

"I'm not sure, but my manager said this group gives charity performances across the region. They have appearances scheduled at nursing homes and hospitals."

Great, just great. If she didn't let them have her van, the entire state of Washington would be filled with disappointed children and old people, and it would be all her fault.

"In other words, if we could find a way to get you to Leavenworth, you'd be willing to relinquish the van?" Theresa sounded optimistic. "Let me find out if that's doable."

Faith waited some more while the clerk explained the situation. The young woman had an expressive face. Her eyes brightened as she glanced at Faith and smiled. Cupping her hand over the receiver, she said, "My manager's talking to the actors now, but it seems their next performance is in the general vicinity of Leavenworth."

"So they could drive me there?"

Theresa nodded. "They can drop you off." She smiled again. "My manager said if you agree to this, she'll personally make sure there's a car available for you later, so you can get back to Seattle."

"Okay." This was becoming a bit complicated, but she was willing to cooperate.

"She also wanted me to tell you that because you're being so great about all of this, there won't be any charge for whatever length of time you have one of our cars."

"Perfect." Faith was pretty sure the rental agency must be desperate to ask such a favor of her. Still, it was Christmas, a time for goodwill.

Theresa's attention returned to the phone. "That'll work. Great. Great."

Fifteen minutes later, Faith was driven to the off-site rental facility. Clasping her paperwork and pulling her suitcase, she half-carried, half-dragged her carry-on bag.

"Can I help you?" a dwarf asked.

"I'm fine, but thank you," she responded, a little startled.

"I think you must be the woman the agency told us about."

"Us?"

"The others are inside."

"The actors?"

"Santa and six elves. I'm one of the elves."

Faith grinned and, bending slightly forward, offered the man her hand. "Faith."

"Tony."

Soon Faith was surrounded by the five other elves and Santa himself. The actors were delightful. Tony introduced each one to Faith. There was Sam, who played the role of Santa. He was, not surprisingly, a full two feet taller than the other cast members, and he had a full white beard and a white head of hair. He must pad his costume because he was trim and didn't look to be more than fifty. His helpers, all dwarfs, were Allen, Norman, Betty, Erica and David. And Tony, of course. Before Faith had an opportunity to repeat their names in her mind, the luggage was transferred from the company van to the rental.

"We sure appreciate this," Sam told her as he slid into the driver's seat.

"I'm happy to help," Faith said, and she meant it.

At Sam's invitation, seconded by Tony, Allen and the others, Faith joined him up front; the six elves took the two rear seats.

"Is Leavenworth out of your way?" she asked.

Sam shook his head. "A little, but you won't hear me complaining." He glanced over at Faith. "We have a performance this afternoon in north Seattle at a children's hospital. If you need to be in Leavenworth before tonight, I could let you take the van with Tony. He has a license, but—"

Theresa hadn't mentioned a performance that day,

but then she probably hadn't known about it either. Faith hesitated. No doubt Tony should be there for the show. Yes, she was tired and yes, she wanted to see her friend, but nothing was so pressing that she had to be in Leavenworth before five that evening.

"I'm surprising a friend," she admitted. "Emily isn't expecting me. So I don't have to get there at any particular time."

"You mean she doesn't even know you're coming?"

"Nope." Faith nearly giggled in her excitement. "She's going to be so happy to see me."

"Then you don't mind attending the performance with us?"

"Not at all." Although she was eager to get to Leavenworth, Faith didn't feel she could deprive children of meeting Tony.

As it turned out, Faith was completely charmed by the performance. Santa and his helpers were wonderful with the sick children, and Tony even enlisted her to assist in the distribution of gifts. The performance was clearly the highlight of their Christmas celebration.

It wasn't until after four that they all piled back into the van. The elves chatted away, pleased everything had gone so well. Faith learned that Sam and his friends had been doing these charity performances for years. They all worked regularly as actors—with roles in movies, TV productions and commercials—

but they took a break at Christmas to bring a bit of joy and laughter into the lives of sick children and lonely old people. Faith felt honored to have been part of it.

"I'm starving," Allen announced not long after they got on the freeway.

Erica and David chimed in. "Me, too."

Not wanting to show up at Emily's hungry, she agreed that they should stop for hamburgers and coffee. Sam insisted on paying for Faith's meal.

"You guys were just great," she said again, biting into her cheeseburger with extra pickles. Emily was going to love them, especially when she learned that they were performing at children's hospitals and retirement homes.

"Thanks."

"What's on the agenda for tomorrow?"

"We aren't due in Spokane until three," Sam told her.

Spokane was a long drive from Leavenworth, and they'd be driving at night. "Do you have hotel reservations?" Faith asked.

"Not until tomorrow," Sam confessed. "Our original plan was to spend the night in Ellensburg."

Faith mulled over this information and knew Emily would encourage her to ask her newfound friends to stay at the house overnight. The place had two extra bedrooms that were rarely used.

"Listen, I'll need to talk it over with my friend, but I'm sure she'd want me to invite you to spend the night." She grinned. "What if you all arrived in costume? I'll be her Christmas surprise—delivered by Santa and his elves. Are you game?"

"You bet," Sam said, and his six friends nodded their agreement.

They all scrambled back into the van, and Tony chuckled from the back seat. "One Christmas delivery, coming right up."

Chapter Eight

Emily was bored and sad and struggling not to break down. There was only one thing left to do—what she always did when she got depressed.

Bake cookies.

But even this traditional cure required a monumental effort. First, she had to locate a grocery store and because she didn't have a car, she'd have to haul everything to the condominium on her own. This was no easy task when she had to buy both flour and sugar. By the time she let herself back into the condo with three heavy bags, she was exhausted.

On the off-chance that she might be able to reach Faith, she tried phoning again. After leaving six messages, Emily knew that if her friend was available, she would've returned the call by now. Faith must be at her sister's because she certainly wasn't at home.

Heather's roommate had apparently left town, too, because there was no answer at the dorm. Emily had to accept that she was alone and friendless in a strange city.

Once she began her baking project, though, her mood improved. She doubted Charles had so much as turned on the oven. In order to bake cookies, she'd had to purchase every single item, including measuring cups and cookie sheets. Once the cookies were ready, Emily knew she couldn't possibly eat them all. It was the baking, not the eating, that she found therapeutic. She intended to pack his freezer with dozens of chocolate chip cookies.

Soon the condo smelled delectable—of chocolate and vanilla and warm cookies. She felt better just inhaling the aroma. As she started sorting through her Christmas CDs, she was startled to hear someone knocking at the door. So far she hadn't met a single other person in the entire building. Her heart hammered with excitement. Really, it was ridiculous to be this thrilled over what was probably someone arriving at her door—Charles's door—by mistake.

Emily squinted through the peephole and saw a man in a wool overcoat and scarf standing in the hallway. He must be a friend of Professor Brewster's, she decided. A rather attractive one with appealing brown eyes and a thick head of hair, or what she could see of his hair. She opened the door.

All he did was stare at her.

Emily supposed she must look a sight. With no apron to be found, she'd tucked a dish towel in the waistband of her jeans. Her Rudolph sweatshirt, complete with blinking red nose, had been a gift from her daughter the year before. She wore fuzzy pink slippers and no makeup.

"Can I help you?"

"Where's Charles?" he asked abruptly.

"And you are?"

"His brother, Ray."

"Oh…" Emily moved aside. "You'd better come in because this is a rather long story."

"It would seem so." He removed his scarf and stepped into the apartment. As soon as he did, he paused and looked around. "This *is* my brother's place?"

"Technically yes, but for the next two weeks it's mine. I'm Emily Springer, by the way."

"Hmm. I hardly recognized it." Ray glanced at the mantel where Emily had hung the two Christmas stockings and put the angel. "Would you mind if I sat down?"

"No. Please do." She gestured toward the low-slung leather chair that resembled something one would find on a beach.

Ray claimed the chair and seemed as uncomfortable as she'd been when she'd tried watching television in it.

"You might prefer the sofa," she said, although that meant they'd be sitting next to each other.

"I think I'll try it." He had to brace his hand on the floor before he could lever himself out of the chair. He stood, sniffed the air and asked, "Are you baking cookies?"

She nodded. "Chocolate chip."

"From scratch?"

Again she nodded. "Would you like some? I've got coffee on, too."

"Not yet." He shook his head. "I think you'd better tell me what's going on with my brother first."

"Yes, of course." Emily sat on the other end of the sofa, and turned sideways, knees together, hands clasped. She just hoped she could get through this without breaking into tears. "It all started when my daughter phoned to say she wouldn't be home for Christmas."

"Your daughter lives here in Boston?"

"Yes." Emily moistened her lips. "Heather attends Harvard." She resisted the urge to brag about Heather's scholarship.

"One of my brother's students?"

The thought had never occurred to Emily. "I don't think so, but I don't know." Apparently there was a lot she didn't know about her daughter's life.

"When I learned that Heather wouldn't be coming home for the holidays, I made the foolish decision to come to Boston, only I couldn't afford more than the airfare."

"In other words, you needed a place to stay?"

"Exactly, so I posted a message on a home-exchange site. Charles contacted me and we exchanged e-mails and decided to trade places for two weeks."

"My brother hates Christmas—that's why he wanted out of the city."

Emily's gaze shot to his. "He didn't mention that."

"Well, it's another long story."

"Then I'm afraid Leavenworth's going to be a bit of a shock."

"Explain that later."

"There's not much more to tell you. Charles is living in my home in Leavenworth, Washington, for the next two weeks and I'm here." She stopped to take a deep breath. "And Heather, my daughter, is in Florida with a man who looks like he might belong to the Hells Angels."

"I see."

Emily doubted that, but didn't say so. "Did Charles know you were coming?"

"No. Actually, my mother asked me to visit. She called and you obviously answered the phone. Mother was convinced something had happened to Charles—that he'd gotten involved with some woman and... Never mind. But she insisted I get over here to, uh, investigate the situation."

"She'll be relieved."

"True," Ray said, "but truth be known, I'm a bit disappointed. It would do my brother a world of good to fall in love."

He didn't elaborate and she didn't question him further. Everything she knew about Charles had come from their e-mail chats, which had been brief and businesslike.

Emily stood and walked into the kitchen. Ray followed her. "So you're alone in the city over Christmas?"

She nodded, forcing a smile. "It isn't exactly what I intended, but there's no going back now." Her home was occupied, and getting a flight out of Boston at this late date was financially unfeasible. She was stuck.

"Listen," Ray said, reaching for a cookie. "Why don't I take you to dinner tonight?"

Emily realized she shouldn't analyze this invitation too closely. Still, she had to know. "Why?"

"Well, because we both need to eat and I'd rather

have a meal with you than alone." He paused to take a bite of the cookie, moaning happily at the taste. "Delicious. Uh—I didn't mean to sound ungracious. Let me try that again. Would you be so kind as to join me for dinner?"

"I'd love to," Emily said, her spirits lifting.

"I'll catch the last train back to New York, explain everything to my mother in the morning and we'll leave it at that. Now, may I have another one of these incomparable cookies?"

"Of course." Emily met his eyes and smiled. He was a likeable man, and at the moment she was in need of a friend. "When would you like to leave?"

Ray checked his watch. "It's six-thirty, so any time is fine with me."

"I'd better change clothes." She pulled the towel free of her waistband, folded it and set it on the kitchen counter.

"Before you do," Ray said stopping her. "Explain what you meant about my brother being in trouble if he isn't fond of Christmas."

"Oh, that." A giggle bubbled up inside her as she told him about Leavenworth in December—the horse-drawn sleigh, the carolers and the three separate tree-lighting ceremonies, one for every weekend before Christmas.

Ray was soon laughing so hard he was wiping

tears from his eyes. Just seeing his amusement made her laugh, too, although she didn't really understand what he found so hilarious.

"If only...if only you knew my b-brother," Ray sputtered. "I can just imagine what he thought when he arrived."

"I guess Charles and I both had the wrong idea about trading homes."

"Sure seems that way," Ray agreed, still grinning. "Why don't I have another cookie while you get ready," he said cheerfully. "I haven't looked forward to a dinner this much in ages."

Come to think of it, neither had Emily.

Chapter Nine

Charles worked at his laptop computer until late in the afternoon. He stopped only when his stomach started to growl. He was making progress and felt good about what he'd managed to accomplish, but he needed a break.

After closing down his computer, he wandered into the kitchen. An inspection of the cupboards and the freezer revealed a wide selection of choices, but he remembered his agreement with Emily. They were to purchase their own food. Emily had been kind enough to prepare yesterday's dinner for him, but he needed to fend for himself from here on out.

There was no help for it; he'd have to venture outside the comfort and security of Emily's house. He'd have to leave this rather agreeable prison and take his chances among the townspeople. The thought sent a chill down his spine.

Peeking through the drapes, Charles rolled his eyes. He was convinced that if he looked hard enough, he'd see Ebeneezer Scrooge and the ghost of Marley, not to mention Tiny Tim hobbling down the sidewalk, complete with his crutch, and crying out, "God bless us everyone."

Once he'd donned his long wool coat and draped a scarf around his neck, he dashed out the door. He locked it behind him, although he wondered why he bothered. According to the kid next door, the entire town knew where Emily kept the key. Still, Charles wanted it understood that he wasn't receiving company.

Walking to his rental car, he hurriedly unlocked it and climbed inside before anyone could stop him. With a sense of accomplishment, he drove until he discovered a large chain grocery store. The lot was full, and there appeared to be some sort of activity taking place in front of the store.

Ducking his head against the wind, he walked rapidly across the parking lot toward the entrance.

A crowd had gathered, and Charles glanced over, wondering at all the commotion. He blinked several times as the scene unfolded before him. Apparently the local church was putting on a Nativity pageant, complete with livestock—a donkey, a goat and several sheep.

Just as he scurried by, the goat raised its head and grabbed the hem of his overcoat. Charles took two steps and was jerked back.

The goat was eating his coat. Apparently no one noticed because the three wise men had decided to make an appearance at the same time. Charles tried to jerk his hem free, but the goat had taken a liking to it and refused to let go. Not wanting to call attention to himself, he decided to ignore the goat and proceed into the store, tugging at his coat as he walked. Unfortunately the goat walked right along behind him, chewing contentedly.

Charles had hoped to dash in, collect his groceries and get out, all in fifteen minutes or less. Instead, everyone in the entire store turned to stare at him as he stumbled in, towing the goat.

"Mister, you've got a goat following you." Some kid, about five or six, was kind enough to point this out, as if Charles hadn't been aware of it.

"Go away." Charles attempted to shoo the goat, but the creature was clearly more interested in its evening meal than in listening to him.

"Oh, sorry." A teenage boy raced after him and

took hold of the goat by the collar. After several embarrassing seconds, the boy managed to get the goat to release Charles's coat.

Before he drew even more attention, Charles grabbed a cart and galloped down the aisles, throwing in what he needed. He paused to gather up the back of his expensive wool coat, which was damp at the hem and looking decidedly nibbled, then with a sigh dropped it again. As he went on his way, he noticed several shoppers who stopped and stared at him, but he ignored them.

He approached the dairy case. As he reached for a quart of milk a barbershop quartet strolled up to serenade him with Christmas carols. Charles listened politely for all of five seconds, then zoomed into a check-out line.

Was there no escape?

By the time he'd loaded his groceries in the car and returned to Emily's home, he felt as if he'd completed the Boston marathon. Now he had to make it from the car to the house undetected.

He looked around to see if any of the neighborhood kids were in sight. He was out of luck, because he immediately caught sight of six or seven of the little darlings, building a snowman in the yard directly next to his.

They all gaped at him.

Charles figured he had only a fifty-fifty chance of making it to the house minus an entourage.

"Hello, mister."

They were already greeting him and he didn't even have the car door completely open. He pretended not to hear them.

"Want to build a snowman with us?"

"No." He scooped up as many of the grocery bags as he could carry and headed toward the house.

"Need help with that?" All the kids raced to his vehicle, eager to offer assistance.

"No."

"You sure?"

"What I want is to be left alone." Charles didn't mean to be rude, but all this Christmas stuff had put him on edge.

The children stared up at him, openmouthed, as if no one had ever said that to them in their entire lives. The little girl blinked back tears.

"Oh, all right," he muttered, surrendering to guilt. He hadn't intended to be unfriendly—it was just that he'd had about as much of this peace and goodwill business as a man could swallow.

The children gleefully tracked through the house, bringing in his groceries and placing them in the kitchen. They looked pleased when they'd finished.

Everyone, that is, except the youngest—Sarah, wasn't it?

"I think someone tried to eat your coat," the little girl said.

"A goat did."

"Must've been Clara Belle," her oldest brother put in. "She's Ronny's 4-H project. He said that goat would latch on to anything. I guess he was right."

Charles grunted agreement and got out his wallet to pay the youngsters.

"You don't have to pay us," the boy said. "We were just being neighborly."

That "neighborly" nonsense again. Charles wanted to argue, but they were out the door before he had a chance to object.

Once Charles had a chance to unpack his groceries and eat, he felt almost human again. He opened the curtains and looked out the window, chuckling at the Kennedy kids' anatomically correct snowman. He wondered what his mother would've said had he used the carrot for anything other than the nose.

It was dark now, and the lights were fast appearing, so Charles shut the curtains again. He considered returning to work. Instead he yawned and decided to take a shower in the downstairs bathroom. He thought he heard something when he got under the spray, but when he listened intently, everything was silent.

Then the sound came again. Troubled now, he turned off the water and yanked a towel from the rack. Wrapping it around his waist, he opened the bathroom door and peered out. He was just about to ask if anyone was there when he heard a female voice.

"Emily? Where are you?" the voice shouted.

Charles gasped and quickly closed the door. He dressed as fast as possible, which was difficult because he was still wet. Zipping up his pants, he stepped out of the bathroom, hair dripping, and came face to face with—Santa Claus.

Both men shouted in alarm.

"Who the hell are you?" Santa cried.

"What are you doing in my house?" Charles demanded.

"Faith!" Santa shouted.

A woman rounded the corner and dashed into the hallway—then stopped dead in her tracks. Her mouth fell open.

"Who are *you?*" Charles shrieked.

"Faith Kerrigan. What have you done with my friend?"

"If you mean Emily Springer, she's in Boston."

"What?" For a moment it looked as if she was about to collapse.

Immediately six elves appeared, all in pointed hats and shoes, crowding the hallway.

Santa and six elves? Charles had taken as much as a Christmas-hating individual could stand. "What the hell is going on here?" he yelled, his patience gone.

"I...I flew in from the Bay area to surprise my friend for Christmas. She didn't say anything about going to Boston."

"We traded houses for two weeks."

"Oh...no." Faith slouched against the wall.

All six of the elves rushed forward to comfort her. Santa looked like he wanted to punch Charles out.

Charles ran his hand down his face. "Apparently there's been...a misunderstanding."

"Apparently," Faith cried as if that was the understatement of the century.

The doorbell chimed, and when Charles went to answer it, the Kennedy kids rushed past him and over to Faith. Their arms went around her waist and they all started to chatter at once, telling her about Heather not coming home and Emily going to Boston.

Adding to the mass confusion were the six elves, who seemed to be arguing among themselves about which one of them would have the privilege of bashing in Charles's nose.

Charles's head started to swim. He raised his arms and shouted in his loudest voice, "Everyone out!"

The room instantly went silent. "Out?" Faith cried.

"We don't have anywhere to go. There isn't a hotel room between here and Spokane with a vacancy now."

Charles slumped onto the arm of the sofa and pressed his hand against his forehead.

"Where do you expect us to go?" Faith asked. Her voice was just short of hysterical. "I've only had a few hours' sleep and my friends changed their plans to drive me to Leavenworth and the van broke down and now—this."

"All right, all right." Charles decided he could bear it for one night as long as everyone left by morning.

The small group looked expectantly at him. "You can spend the night—but just tonight. Tomorrow morning, all of you are out of here. Is that understood?"

"Perfectly," Faith answered on their behalf.

Not a one of them looked grateful enough. "Count your blessings," Charles snapped.

Really, he had no other choice—besides kicking them out into the cold.

"Thank you," Faith whispered, looking pale and shaken.

Charles glared at the mixed ensemble of characters. Santa, elves, kids and a surprisingly attractive woman stared back at him. "Remember, tomorrow morning you're gone. All of you."

Faith nodded and led Santa and his elves up the stairs.

"Good." First thing in the morning, all these people would be out of this house and out of his life.

Or so Charles hoped. He didn't have the energy to wonder why the tall guy and the six short ones were all in Christmas costume.

Chapter Ten

Early in the evening, Emily and Ray left the condominium. Although it was dark, Ray insisted on showing her the waterfront area. They walked for what seemed like miles, talking and laughing. Ray was a wonderful tour guide, showing her Paul Revere's house and the site of the Boston Tea Party. Both were favorites of his brother's, he pointed out, telling her proudly of Charles's accomplishments as a historian. From the harbor they strolled through St. Stephen's Church and Copp's Hill Burying Ground, which began in 1659 and was the city's second-oldest graveyard. They strolled from one site to the next. Time flew, and when Emily glanced at her watch, she was astonished to discover it was almost eight-thirty.

On Hanover Street, they stopped for dinner at one of Ray's favorite Italian restaurants. The waiter seated them at a corner table and even before handing them menus, he delivered a large piece of cheese and a crusty loaf of warm bread with olive oil for dipping.

"Have I completely worn you out?" Ray asked, smiling over at Emily. He started to peruse the wine list, which had been set in front of him.

Yes, she was tired, but it was a nice kind of tired. "No, quite the contrary. Oh, Ray, thank you so much."

He looked up, obviously surprised.

"A few hours ago, I was feeling utterly sorry for myself. I was staying in one of the most historic cities in our country and all I could think about was how miserable I felt. And right outside my door was all this." She made a wide sweeping gesture with her arm. "I can't thank you enough for opening my eyes to Boston."

He smiled again—and again she was struck by what a fine-looking man he was.

"The pleasure was all mine," he told her softly.

The waiter came with their water glasses and menus. By now, Emily was hungry, and after slicing off pieces of cheese for herself and for Ray, she studied the menu. Ray closed the wine list. After consulting with her, he ordered a bottle of Chianti and an antipasto dish.

As soon as the waiter took their dinner order, Ray

leaned back in his seat and reached inside his suit jacket for his cell phone.

"I'd better give my mother a call. I was planning to do it tomorrow, but knowing her, she's waiting anxiously to hear about the strange woman who's corrupted her son."

"You or Charles?" Emily teased.

Ray grinned and punched out a single digit. He raised the small phone to his ear. "Hello, Mother."

His smile widened as he listened for a long moment. "I have someone with me I'd like you to meet."

He had to pause again, listening to his mother's lengthy response.

"Yes, this is the evil woman you feared had ruined your son. She might still do it, too."

"Stop it," Emily mouthed and gently kicked his shoe beneath the table.

"Not to worry—Charles is in Washington State. Here, I'll let Emily explain everything." He handed her the cell phone.

Emily had barely gotten the receiver to her ear when she heard the woman on the other end of the line demand, "To whom am I speaking?"

"Mrs. Brewster, my name is Emily Springer, and Charles and I traded homes for two weeks."

"You're living in Charles's condo?" She didn't seem to believe Emily.

"Yes, but just until after Christmas."

"Oh."

"Charles and I met over the Internet at a site set up for this type of exchange."

"I see." The woman went suspiciously silent.

"It's only for two weeks."

"You're telling me my son let you move into his home sight unseen? And that, furthermore, Charles has ventured all the way to the West Coast?" The question sounded as if it came from a prosecuting attorney who'd found undeniable evidence of perjury.

"Yes… I came to Boston to see my daughter." For the last few days, Emily had tried not to think about Heather, which was nearly impossible.

"Let me speak to Rayburn," his mother said next.

Emily handed the cell phone back to Ray.

Ray and his mother chatted for another few minutes before he closed the phone and stuck it inside his pocket.

By then the wine had been delivered and poured. Emily reached for her glass and sipped. She enjoyed wine on occasion, but this was a much finer quality than she normally drank.

"Rayburn?" she said, teasing him by using the same tone his mother had used.

He groaned. "If you think that's bad, my little brother's given name is actually Hadley."

"Hadley?"

"Hadley Charles. The minute he was old enough to speak, he refused to let anyone call him Hadley."

Emily smiled. "I can't say I blame him."

"Rayburn isn't much of an improvement."

"No, but it's better than Hadley."

"That depends." Ray sipped his wine and sat up straighter when the waiter brought the antipasto plate. It was a meal unto itself, with several varieties of sliced meats, cheese, olives and roasted peppers.

That course was followed by soup and then pasta. Emily was convinced she couldn't swallow another bite when the main course, a cheese-stuffed chicken dish, was brought out.

When they'd finished, they lingered over another bottle of wine. Ray leaned forward, elbows resting on the table, and they talked, moving from one subject to the next. Emily had hardly ever met a man who was so easy to talk to. He seemed knowledgeable about any number of subjects.

"You're divorced?" he asked, as they turned to more personal matters.

"Widowed. Eleven years ago. Peter was killed when Heather was just a little girl."

"I'm sorry."

"Thank you." She could speak of Peter now without pain, but that had taken years. She was a different woman than she'd been back then, as a young wife and mother. "Peter was a good husband and a wonderful father. I still miss him."

"Is there a reason you've never remarried?"

"Not really. I got caught up in Heather's life and my job. Over the years I've dated now and then, but there was never any spark. What about you?"

He shrugged. "I've been consumed by my job for so long, I don't know what it is to have an ordinary life."

This interested Emily. "I've always wondered what an ordinary life would be like. Does anyone really have one?"

"Good point."

"Did you have any important relationships?"

"I dated quite a bit when I was in my twenties and early thirties. I became seriously involved twice, but both times I realized, almost from the first, that it wouldn't last."

"Sounds like a self-fulfilling prophecy to me."

He grinned as he picked up his wineglass. "My mother said almost those identical words to me. The thing is, I admired both women and, to some extent loved them, but deep down I suspect they knew it wouldn't last, either."

"And it didn't."

"Right. I put long hours into my job and I have a lot

of responsibilities. I love publishing. No one's more excited than I am when one of our authors does well."

Emily had plenty of questions about the publishing world, but she knew Ray must have been asked these same questions dozens of times. They had this one evening together, and Emily didn't want to bore him with idle curiosity.

When they'd finished the second bottle of wine, Emily felt mellow and sleepy. Most of the other tables were vacant, and the crew of waiters had started changing tablecloths and refilling the salt and pepper shakers.

Ray noticed the activity going on around them, too. "What time is it?" he asked, sitting up and glancing at his watch with an unbelieving expression.

"It's ten to eleven."

"You're kidding!" He looked shocked.

"Well, you know what they say about time flying, etc."

He chuckled softly. "Tonight certainly was an enjoyable evening—but there's a problem."

"Oh?"

He downed the last of his wine and announced, "I'm afraid the next train doesn't leave for New York until tomorrow morning."

"Oh…right." Emily had entirely forgotten that Ray would have to catch the train.

He relaxed visibly, apparently finding a solution to his problem. "Not to worry, I'll get a hotel room. That shouldn't be too difficult."

Without a reservation, she wondered if that was true. Furthermore, she hated the thought of him spending that extra money on her account. "You don't need to do that."

"What do you mean?"

"Your brother's condo has two bedrooms."

He raised his eyebrows.

"I'm sleeping in the guest room, and I'm sure your brother wouldn't object to your taking his room."

Ray hesitated and looked uncertain. "Are you sure you're comfortable with that arrangement?"

"Of course."

That was easy to say after two bottles of wine. Had Emily been completely sober, she might not have—but really, what could it hurt?

She decided that question was best left unanswered.

Chapter Eleven

Heather Springer wrapped her arms tightly around Elijah's waist, the sound of the wind roaring in her ears. She laid her head against his muscular back and relished the feel of his firm body so close to her own. Three other Harleys, all with passengers, zoomed down the Interstate on their way to the white sandy beaches of Florida.

Try as she might, Heather couldn't stop thinking about the bewildered look on her mother's face when she learned Heather had made her own plans for the Christmas holidays.

The least her mother could've done was let her know she was flying to Boston. It was supposed to be a big surprise—well, it definitely was that. Actually, it was more of a shock, and not a pleasant one. Heather had hoped for the proper time to tell her mother about Elijah. That opportunity, unfortunately, had been taken away from her.

Heather sighed. She was grateful when Elijah pulled into a rest area near Daytona Beach. He climbed off the Harley and removed his helmet, shaking his head to release his long hair.

Heather watched as the other motorcycles pulled into nearby spaces. Heather was proud that Elijah led the way in this adventure. Being with him during the holidays was thrilling, and she wasn't about to let her stick-in-the-mud, old-fashioned mother ruin it.

Elijah was different from any boy Heather had ever dated. The others paled by comparison, especially Ben who was traditional and frankly boring. All he thought about was school and work and getting his law degree. For once, just once, she wanted to think about something besides grades and scholarship money. She wanted to *live*.

She'd met Elijah at Starbucks, and they'd struck up a conversation. That was in early October, and after meeting him everything had changed. Never before had she been in love like this. It was exciting and crazy and new. Elijah's world was completely unlike her own, and she knew their differences were what made him so attractive. He was dark, wild, dangerous—all she'd ever craved. She wanted to share his life, share everything with him. Heather felt pleased that he was introducing her to his friends, but she'd noticed he wasn't interested in meeting hers. That hadn't bothered her until recently. Heather didn't know the other bikers and their girlfriends very well, but she liked them and hoped for the chance to connect.

"Feel that sunshine," Elijah said. He closed his eyes and tilted his face toward the sun.

Heather removed her own helmet and slid off the Harley. "It's not as warm as I thought it would be." She didn't want to complain, but she'd assumed the temperature would be in the seventies; it was closer to the fifties. This wasn't exactly swimming-in-the-ocean kind of weather.

"Once we're in the Miami Beach area you'll be hot enough," Elijah promised. "Until then I'll keep you warm." He circled her waist with his massive arms.

She turned in his embrace, kissing him lightly.

"I thought we'd hang out here for a while," he murmured.

"That sounds good to me." Heather didn't want to admit how much her backside ached, especially when the others didn't seem to have any such complaint. She'd heard one of the girls comment that Heather was walking oddly and then giggle. Heather pretended not to hear. She wasn't one of them, but she badly wanted to be. Given a chance, she'd prove herself, she vowed.

Soon the eight of them were sprawled out on the grass. Elijah lay on his back, his head resting on Heather's lap. She sat leaning against a palm tree.

"You okay?" Elijah asked.

"Of course." She tried to make light of her feelings, rather than confess what she was really thinking.

"You've been pretty quiet."

Heather slipped her fingers through his hair. "I suppose."

"I bet it's your mother."

Heather sighed and realized she couldn't hide her thoughts any longer. "She might've said something, you know."

Elijah nodded. "You couldn't have known she was planning to fly in for Christmas."

Heather twirled a lock of his dark hair around her finger. "She didn't even hint at her plans. It's like she expected me to abandon everything just because she showed up in Boston."

"Parents are unreasonable."

"Yeah." Still, the sick feeling in the pit of her stomach refused to go away.

"It's better with just you and me," he whispered.

Heather didn't bother to mention that there were three other couples tagging along. In the beginning, it was supposed to be just the two of them. But as soon as word got out, several of Elijah's friends had asked to join them. He'd agreed without discussing it with Heather. She hadn't said anything, but she was disappointed.

She'd had their first Christmas together all planned out. Once they reached Miami or the Keys, she'd make this Christmas as special for him as her mother had always made the holiday for her. They'd decorate a tree, sing carols on the beach and open small gifts to each other.

Thinking about her mother depressed her.

"You've got that look again," Elijah muttered, frowning up at her.

"Sorry."

"Forget about her, okay?"

"I'm trying, but it's hard. I wonder what she's doing and who she's with." The thought of her mother all alone tugged at Heather's heart, and despite her best efforts, she couldn't stop feeling guilty. She steeled herself against those emotions. If anyone was to blame for this fiasco, it was her mother, not her!

"You've got to let go of this, or it'll ruin everything," Elijah warned.

"I know."

"You said you and your mother were tight."

"We used to be." Heather knew that nothing

would be the same again, and she was glad, she told herself fiercely. Well, maybe not glad exactly, but relieved that her mother knew about Elijah.

"It's time she understood that you're your own woman and you make your own decisions."

Elijah was repeating the same things she'd told her mother, the same things she'd been saying to herself from the moment they left Boston. "You're right."

"Of course I'm right. She can't dictate to you anymore, you know."

Heather agreed in principle, but that didn't do a thing to ease the knot in her stomach. "I'd feel better if I talked to her."

"You already did."

That was true, but Heather had lingering doubts about their conversation. She'd been shocked and angry when she'd learned her mother was in town. Everything she'd worked toward all these weeks was in danger, and she refused to let her mother ruin her plans.

Elijah studied her, his gaze narrowed. "You've changed your mind, haven't you?"

"About what? Us?" Heather pressed her hands gently against the sides of Elijah's bearded face and stared down at him, letting her love for him fill her eyes. "Oh, Elijah, about us? Never." As if to prove her undying love and devotion, she lowered her mouth to his.

Elijah was a seductive kisser, and he brought his muscular arms around her neck and half lifted his head to meet her lips. His mouth was moist and sensual and before long, any thoughts of her mother vanished completely.

When Elijah released her, Heather kept her eyes closed and sighed softly.

"Are you still worried about your mother?" he teased.

"Mother? What mother?"

Elijah chuckled. "That's what I figured."

Oh, how she loved her motorcycle man.

"You ready to go?" he asked.

The prospect of climbing back on the Harley didn't thrill her, but she tried to sound enthusiastic. "Anytime you say."

Elijah rewarded her with a smile. "And the guys said you'd be trouble."

"Me?"

"College girls generally are."

"So I'm not your first college girl?"

He laughed, but the sound lacked amusement. "I've been around."

She ignored that. She didn't want to hear about any of his other women, because she was determined it would be different with her.

They were good for each other. With Elijah she

could throw away her good-girl image and discover her real self. At the same time, she'd teach him about love and responsibility. She didn't know exactly how he made his money, although he always seemed to have enough for gas and beer. But Heather wasn't concerned about that right now; she was determined to enjoy herself.

In one graceful movement Elijah leaped to his feet and stood. As soon as he was upright, the others started to move, too. He was their unspoken leader, their guide to adventure. And Heather was his woman, and she loved it.

Elijah offered Heather his hand, which she took. She brushed the grass and grit from her rear and started back across the grass and the parking lot to where he'd parked the Harley.

Elijah gave Heather her helmet. "You don't need to feel guilty about your mother," he said.

"I don't." But she did. "Still, I think I should call her."

"I thought you said she doesn't have a cell phone."

"She doesn't."

"Do you know where she's staying?"

"No…but—"

"It's out of the question, then, isn't it?"

Heather was forced to agree. Even if she wanted to, she realized in an instant of panic, she had no way of reaching her mother.

Chapter Twelve

"*How* much?" Faith Kerrigan couldn't believe what the airline representative on the phone was telling her. According to what he said, her flight back to California would cost nearly twice as much as her original ticket.

"That's if I can find you a seat," he added.

"Oh." Faith could feel a headache coming on. She pressed her fingertips to her temple, which didn't help.

"Do you want me to check for an available flight?" the man asked.

"I—no." Her other option was to wait until there was a rental car available, with a different agency if necessary, and then drive back to California. The fees couldn't possibly be as steep as what the airlines wanted to charge. One thing was certain—she couldn't stay in Leavenworth. She hauled out Emily's phone book and began to call the local car rental places.

This entire Christmas was a disaster. If only she'd talked to Emily before she booked her flight. Oh no, she groaned to herself, that would have been far too sensible. She'd wanted to surprise her friend. Some surprise! Instead, *she* was the one who'd gotten the shock of her life.

Sam, Tony and the other dwarfs tiptoed around the house as quietly as possible, not wanting to intrude on the curmudgeon. What an unlikable fellow he was! But at least he'd been kind enough not to cast them into the cold dark night. She reminded herself that he'd only delayed it until morning—which made it difficult to maintain much gratitude.

Faith hadn't seen Charles yet. The den door was closed and she could only assume he was on his computer, doing whatever it was he found so important.

"It's time we left," Sam announced once she was off the phone.

Faith still didn't know what she'd do, but the problem was hers and hers alone. Santa and the small troupe of dwarfs gathered around and watched her with anxious expressions.

"Are you sure you'll be safe with *him?*" Tony motioned toward the closed door. Judging by the intense look he wore, he seemed to welcome the opportunity to share his opinion of Charles—with Charles himself.

Faith resisted the urge to kiss his forehead for being so sweet. "I'll be perfectly fine, don't you worry." She hoped she sounded more confident than she felt, but she wanted to send her friends off without burdening them with her troubles.

Sam hesitated, as if he wasn't convinced he should believe her. He scratched his white beard, frowning. "You have a way back to California?"

"Not quite, but I'm working on it. I've called the car rental agency, plus several others. I'm waiting to hear back."

Sam's frown deepened. He seemed about to suggest she join them, but Faith knew that would be impossible.

"You go on," she insisted, "and if I run into any trouble, I'll give you a call." She had his cell phone number. Faith still felt his reluctance, but eventually, after conferring with the others, Sam agreed.

Smiling bravely, she stood on the porch and watched as they climbed into the rental van and backed out of the driveway. She waved until they were out of sight. Her heart sank when she could no longer see them. Soon, far sooner than she was ready, she'd be facing Charles with the unwelcome news from the airlines. Perhaps he'd offer a suggestion, but it was all too clear that he wanted her gone.

Already the two oldest Kennedy children were outside, frolicking in the snow. "Wanna go sledding with us?" Thomas called out to her. He walked toward the park, dragging his sled behind him. His younger brother Jimmy followed, tugging his own sled.

"Maybe later," Faith shouted back. She didn't have the heart to tell him she probably wouldn't be in town much longer.

The cold cut through Faith and she rubbed her hands up and down her arms. She hurried back into the warm comfort of the house, leaning against the closed door as she considered her limited options. She was so deep in thought that it took her a moment to notice Charles standing on the far side of the room.

"Santa and his elves have left?" he asked. "Why were they wearing those outfits, anyway?" He sounded both curious and a touch sardonic.

"Oh—we went to a rest stop and they got changed. We decided it would be part of Emily's Christmas surprise."

"Uh huh."

Faith avoided eye contact.

"What about you? You're leaving today, too—aren't you?"

Faith raised her index finger and swallowed. "There's...a small problem."

"How small?"

"Well, actually it's a rather large one." She told him how much it would cost to change her flight.

"*How* much?" He sounded as appalled as she was.

"The way it was explained to me is that this would be a new ticket. But the representative said that even if I was willing to pay the change fee, it was unlikely he could find me a seat. I could fly stand-by, but he told me there are hardly ever any stand-by seats at this time of year." Faith knew she was giving him more information than necessary, but it was critical that he understand her position.

Charles sighed as if this was too much to take in all at once. "Summarize, please," he snapped—as if she was some freshman in one of his classes, she thought resentfully. "Where does that leave you?"

"Well...I have a rental car...or rather I did until Sam and the dwarfs needed it, so I ended up giving it to them." Again she explained far more than necessary, ending with the tale of the troupe's appearances at hospitals and nursing homes.

"So, you're saying they've left with the one and only van?"

She nodded. "I have calls into several rental agencies now, and they're all looking for a car for me. But rest assured that once I do have a vehicle, I'll be out of here."

"Where will you go?"

She didn't have many options there, either. "Back to California."

Charles had the good grace to look concerned. "You'd be driving at this time of year and in this weather?"

"Do I have a choice?"

He sighed, turned abruptly and walked into the kitchen. "Let me think about this. There's got to be a solution that'd suit both of us."

She was glad he seemed to think there were other options, because she couldn't think of any. The one obvious solution—that she simply stay—was as unpalatable to her as it no doubt was to him.

After a few minutes, Charles returned to the den and closed the door. Apparently he hadn't come up with any creative ideas.

Faith's stomach growled, reminding her that she hadn't eaten since yesterday afternoon. Checking out the refrigerator, she found eggs, cheese and a few vegetables. She whipped up two omelets, then timidly knocked at the den door.

At Charles's gruff reply, she creaked open the door just enough to peer inside. "I made breakfast if you're interested."

"Breakfast? Oh. Yeah, sure."

She didn't need to ask him twice. Maybe half a minute later, Charles joined her at the table. He stared down at his plate, eyes widening as if this was the most delicious meal he'd seen in years.

He sat down and sampled the omelet. "You cook like this all the time?"

Faith wasn't sure what he was asking. "I know my way around a kitchen, if that's what you mean," she said cautiously.

"Every meal?"

"Not always, but I do enjoy cooking."

He ate several more bites, pausing between each one, a blissful expression on his face. "You'd be willing to leave me alone to do my work?"

"If that's a question, I suppose I could manage to keep out of your way." She'd begun to feel hopeful— maybe they *could* compromise.

He studied her narrowly, as if to gauge the truth of her words. "In that case you can stay. You prepare the meals, make yourself scarce, and we'll both cope with this as well as we can. Agreed?"

Faith doubted he knew how gruff and unfriendly he sounded. However… "I could do that."

"Good. I'm here to work. The last thing I'm interested in is Christmas or any of the festivities that seem to have taken over this town. Tell me, are these people crazy? No, don't answer that. Just leave me alone—except for meals, of course."

"Fine."

"I want nothing to do with Christmas. Got that?"

"Yes."

She had no idea what kind of work he was doing, but she'd gladly keep her distance. As for the Christmas part, he'd certainly made his point and she didn't need to hear it again.

"I'll probably have my meals in the den."

"Fine," she said again. As far as she was concerned, the less she had to do with him, the better.

Charles set his fork next to his plate and seemed to be waiting for something more from her.

"I'm willing to make the best of this situation if you are," she finally said. Neither was to blame. They were the victims of a set of unfortunate circumstances.

He nodded solemnly as if to seal their agreement. Then he pushed away from the table and stood. "I will tell you that this is one of the best omelets I've had in years."

She smiled, pleased to hear it. "Thank you." Then she hopped up from the table, taking her plate and cup. "What time would you like lunch?"

"I hadn't thought about it."

"Okay, I'll let you know when it's ready. Fair enough?"

"Certainly." He sounded distracted and eager to get back to his work.

"I'll pick up the groceries," she offered. "It's the least I can do."

His eyes brightened. "That would be appreciated. Just be careful of the goat."

"The goat?"

"Never mind," he muttered and returned to the den.

Chapter Thirteen

Bernice Brewster slept well for the first time in three days. At her age, she shouldn't be worrying about her adult children, but Charles was a concern. For that matter, so was Rayburn. Thankfully her older son had taken her apprehensions to heart and traveled to Boston to check on his younger brother.

Naturally there was a perfectly logical explanation as to why a woman had answered Charles's phone. She should've realized her sensible son wouldn't have some stray woman in the house. Charles was far too intelligent to be taken in by a gold digger. Granted, she'd like nothing better than to see him with the right woman—but there'd be nothing worse than seeing him with the wrong one. Like that Monica. Well, she was a fool and didn't deserve Charles.

Fortunately, Bernice now had the phone number in Washington State where Charles could be reached. She leaned toward the telephone and dialed.

One ring. Two.

"Hello," a female voice answered.

"Hello," Bernice responded, a little uncertainly. She must have written the number down incorrectly. There was only one way to find out and that was to ask. "This phone number was given to me by Emily Springer. Is Charles Brewster there?"

The woman hesitated. "Yes, but he's unavailable at the moment."

Bernice swallowed a gasp and before she could think better of it, slammed down the telephone. Dear heaven, what was happening? Feeling light-headed, she waited until her pounding heart had settled down before she tried to call Rayburn at his apartment. She wanted to know what was going on and she wanted to know right this minute.

When Rayburn didn't answer, she tried his office and learned he was still in Boston.

"Why?" she demanded of his assistant. "Why is he still in Boston?"

"I'm sorry, Mrs. Brewster," the young woman said

politely. "Mr. Brewster phoned the office this morning and that's what he said."

"He has his cell phone?" Of course he did, because he'd called her on it the night before.

"I believe he does."

Bernice carefully punched out the cell number and waited. The phone rang four times before her son answered.

"Ray Brewster."

"Rayburn," she gasped, overwhelmed by her children's odd behavior. His greeting had sounded far too friendly, as if he'd been laughing. Well, this was no laughing matter!

"Mother." The sound of her voice sobered him up fast enough, she noticed. Something very suspicious was going on.

"Where *are* you?" she demanded.

"I'm forty-three years old. I no longer need to check in with you."

How dared he speak to her in that tone! She was about to say so when Rayburn chuckled.

"If you must know, I'm in Boston at Charles's condo."

"There's a *woman* there."

"I already know that, Mother."

Bernice gasped. "You spent the night with her?"

"I was in the same condo, not that it's any of your business."

Bernice pulled out her lace-edged hankie and clenched it tightly. "I...I have no idea where your father and I went wrong that both my sons—"

"Mother, take a deep breath and start over."

Bernice tried, she honestly tried, but her heart was pounding and her head spinning. "I phoned the number you gave me and...another woman answered."

"A woman? Are you sure you had the right number?"

"Of course I'm sure. I asked and she said Charles was unavailable."

"Hold on, let me ask Emily who it might be."

Emily, was it? "I see you're on a first-name basis with this—this house-stealer."

To her chagrin, Rayburn laughed. "Honestly, Mother, I think you missed your calling. You should've been on the stage."

Her husband used to make the same claim, and while she did have a good stage presence, she suspected Rayburn didn't mean it as a compliment.

Bernice could hear him in the background, but hard as she pressed her ear against the receiver, she couldn't make out what was being said.

"Emily says she doesn't have a clue who would be answering the phone at her place. She'll call later and find out if you wish."

"If I *wish?*" Bernice repeated.

"All right, I'll get back to you."

Her son was about to hang up, but she still had more to say. "Rayburn," she shouted. "You behave yourself with this woman, understand?"

"Yes, Mother."

The phone line went dead.

"A woman answered?" Emily repeated after Ray ended the conversation with his mother. "Now, that's interesting."

"Who do you think it might be?"

Emily shrugged. "Don't know, but it'll be easy enough to find out." She went to the telephone and punched out her own number in Washington State.

The line was picked up almost right away. "Hello."

"Faith?" Emily shrieked. "Faith? Is it really you?"

"Emily?"

They both started talking at once, blurting out questions and answers, then each explained in turn. Even then, it took Emily a few moments to discern what had actually happened.

"Oh, no! You came to spend Christmas with me and I'm not there."

"You went to Boston to be with Heather and now she's in Florida?"

"Yes, but I can't think about it, otherwise I'll get too upset."

Faith was sympathetic. "I felt so badly for the way I brushed off your disappointment."

"And now you're trapped in Leavenworth."

"There are worse places to be this time of year," Faith said. She seemed to be in a good frame of mind. "Charles and I have reached an agreement," she went on to say. "I'm staying until after Christmas, and in exchange, I'll keep out of his way and cook his meals."

While her friend put a positive slant on the situation, Emily realized Faith had to be miserable. Alone—or virtually alone—at Christmas.

"What about you?" Faith asked.

"I'm stuck in Boston, but it's really a lovely town." Still, none of that mattered now. "Oh, Faith, what a good friend you are to go to all this trouble for me."

"Well, I tried."

Emily wanted to weep. Despite everything, it seemed she was destined to spend the holidays by herself. Still, she'd had a wonderful evening with Ray and felt attractive and carefree in a way she hadn't in years.

They talked for several minutes longer, making plans to call each other again. When she finished, Emily replaced the receiver and looked over at Ray, smiling.

"I take it she's someone you know?"

Emily told him what had happened. "I was lucky I caught her. Faith was on her way outside to go sledding with the neighbor kids. She's so good with children."

"Faith sounds like a fun-loving person."

"She is."

"She's staying, then?"

Emily nodded. "She and Charles have worked out a compromise." Emily felt guilty about the whole mess. Poor Charles. All he wanted was to escape Christmas and have time to work without interruption. But, between Faith and the Kennedy children, Emily figured the poor man wouldn't have a moment's peace.

Ray drank the rest of his coffee and set his mug aside. "I guess I'd better head back to New York."

Emily knew it was too much to hope that he'd stay on. "I can't let you go without breakfast," she said brightly.

Ray seemed almost relieved at being given an excuse to linger. "Are you sure I'm not disrupting your plans?"

"Plans? What plans? I'm here for another week and I don't know a soul in town." She opened the cupboard, looking for ideas, and found an old-fashioned waffle iron. She brought it down, oiled it and plugged it in.

"I wondered what happened to Mom's old waffle iron," Ray said as he leaned against the counter. He watched Emily assemble ingredients.

"Are you hungry?" he asked.

She shrugged as she cracked an egg against the side of the bowl. "Not really... The truth is, I'm just delaying the inevitable." It probably wasn't polite to be this truthful, but she was beyond pretense. The minute Ray walked out that door, she'd be alone again and she'd enjoyed his company.

"Actually, I'm not hungry, either."

"You aren't?" The question came out in a rushed whisper.

Ray shook his head. "I was looking for an excuse to stay."

He and Emily exchanged a grin.

"Do we actually need an excuse?" he asked.

Emily didn't know how to answer or even if she should. "Do you have to go back to New York?"

"At the moment I can't think of a single compelling reason."

"Would you be interested in staying in Boston for Christmas? With me?" Normally she wasn't this direct, but she had little to lose and so much to gain.

"I can't imagine anyone I'd rather spend Christmas with."

Chapter Fourteen

On a mission now, Faith walked down Main Street in Leavenworth and headed for her favorite grocery. Even after a number of years away, she was astonished by the number of people who remembered her. Five years earlier, she'd done her student teaching in Leavenworth and worked in Emily's classroom.

Newly divorced, emotionally fragile and struggling to pick up the pieces of her life, she'd come to this out-of-the-way community. The town had welcomed her, and with Emily as her friend, she'd learned that life does continue.

The three months she'd spent with Emily had been like a reprieve for Faith, providing a much-needed escape from her badly bungled life. Once her student teaching was completed, she'd moved back to Seattle and soon afterward graduated with her master's degree in education. Diploma in hand, she'd gone to California to be closer to family.

Although she'd moved away from Leavenworth, Faith had stayed in contact with Emily. Their friendship had continued to grow, despite the physical distance between them and the difference in their ages. In fact, Faith felt she could talk to Emily in ways she couldn't talk to her mother. They were colleagues, but not only that, they'd both experienced the loss of a marriage, albeit for very different reasons and in very different ways.

They made a point of getting together every summer. Usually they met in Seattle or California. The long-distance aspect of the relationship hadn't been a hindrance.

Faith's family and friends were important to her; romance, though, was another matter. She was rather frightened of it. Her marriage had burned her and while she'd like to be settled and married with children, that didn't seem likely now.

As she walked through town, Faith waved at people she recognized. Some immediately waved back; one woman stopped and stared as if she had yet to place her. The living Nativity wasn't scheduled until the afternoon, so she was safe from the goat Charles had mentioned. She'd figured out that the infamous Clara Belle—she remembered Emily's hilarious story about a farm visit with her kindergarten class—had to be the goat in question.

Thinking of Charles made her smile. He was an interesting character. If he hadn't already told her, she would've guessed he was an academic. He fit the stereotype of the absentminded professor perfectly— a researcher who became so absorbed in his work, he needed someone to tell him when and where he needed to be.

He did have a heart, though. Otherwise she'd probably be hitchhiking back to California by now. As long as she made herself invisible, they would manage.

Once inside the store, she got a grocery cart and wandered aimlessly down the aisle, seeking inspiration for dinner. She decided on baked green peppers stuffed with a rice, tomato soup and ground beef mixture. The recipe was her mother's but Faith rarely made it. Cooking for one was a chore and it was often easier to pick up something on the way home from school. Fresh cranberries were on sale, so she grabbed a package of those, although she hadn't decided what to do with them. It seemed a Christmassy thing to buy. She'd find a use for them later.

She'd come up with menus for the rest of the week this afternoon, and write a more complete grocery list then.

On the walk home, Faith discovered the Kennedy kids and about half the town's children sledding down the big hill in the park. If her arms hadn't been full, she would've stopped and taken a trip down the hill herself.

The kids were so involved in their fun that they didn't notice her. Breathless, Faith brought everything into the kitchen. She removed her hat and gloves and draped her coat over the back of a chair. Unpacking the groceries, she sang a Christmas song that was running through her mind.

The door to the den flew open and Charles stood in the doorway glaring at her.

Faith stopped midway to the refrigerator, a package of ground beef in her hand. "Was I making too much noise?" she asked guiltily. In her own opinion, she'd been quiet and subdued, but apparently not.

"I'm trying to work here," he told her severely.

"Sorry," she mouthed and tiptoed back to the kitchen counter.

"You aren't planning to do anything like bake cookies, are you?" He wrinkled his nose as if to say he wasn't interested.

"Uh, I hadn't given it any thought."

"In case you do, you should know I don't want to be distracted by smells, either."

"Smells?" With an effort, Faith managed not to groan out loud.

"The aroma of baking cookies makes my stomach growl."

He wasn't kidding, and Faith found that humorous, although she dared not show it. She was able to stay here only with his approval and couldn't afford to jeopardize her position. "Then rest assured. I won't do anything to make your stomach growl."

"Good." With that, Charles retreated into the den, closing the door decisively.

Faith rolled her eyes. What was she supposed to do all day? Sit in a corner and knit? Play solitaire? If that little bit of commotion had bothered His Highness, then she couldn't see this arrangement working. And yet, what was the alternative?

The awful part was that she felt an almost overwhelming urge to bang lids together. Standing in the middle of the kitchen, she had to bite her lower lip to restrain herself from singing at the top of her lungs and stomping her feet.

This was crazy. Ludicrous. Still, it was all she could do not to behave in the most infantile manner. If she was going to behave like a child, then she might as well join the children. This close to Christmas, they had a lot of pent-up energy.

Dressed in hat, gloves and her coat once again, Faith went outside. The snow on the front lawn was untouched. A fresh layer had fallen overnight, and with time on her hands, she made an impulsive decision to build a snowman. She grinned as she looked at the speciman in the neighbor's yard.

Starting with a small hand-size ball of snow, she rolled it across the lawn, letting it grow larger and fuller with each sweep.

"Do you want me to help?" Sarah asked, appearing at her side.

Sarah was a favorite of Emily's, Faith knew. As the youngest in a big family, she'd learned to hold her own.

"I sure do."

The little girl beamed as Faith resumed the snow-rolling task. "The bottom part of the snowman has to be the biggest," Sarah pointed out, obviously taking on supervisory responsibilities.

"Right."

"Dylan says it's the most important part, too."

Dylan, if Faith remembered correctly, lived down the street and was a good friend to one of the Kennedy boys.

"Are you building a fort?" Thomas shouted, hurrying across the street from the park. He abandoned his sled near the front porch.

"This is a nice friendly snowman," Faith assured him.

Thomas narrowed his eyes. "Looks more like a snow fort to me."

"It's a ball," Sarah primly informed her brother, hands on her hips. "Anyone can see that."

"I don't think so." Thomas raced over to his own yard and started rolling snow. He was quickly joined by his brothers. The boys worked feverishly at constructing their fort.

Sarah and Faith hurried to catch up, changing their tactics. There were four boys against the two of them, but what they lacked in numbers they made up for in cunning. While Faith built their defensive wall, Sarah rolled snowballs, stacking them in neat piles out of sight of her brothers.

"Now, boys," Faith said, standing up and strolling to the middle of the battleground between their two yards. "I'm telling you right now that it's not a good thing to pick a fight with girls."

"Yeah, because they tattle."

"Do not," Sarah screeched.

"Do, too."

Faith stretched out her arms to silence both sides. "Sarah and I were innocently building a friendly snowman for Mrs. Springer's front yard when we were accused of constructing a snow fort."

"It *is* a snow fort," Thomas insisted, pointing accusingly at the wall of snow.

"It became one when you started building yours," Faith said. "But before we go to war, I feel honor bound to look for some means of making peace."

"No way!" Mark cried.

"Hear me out," Faith urged. "First of all, it's unfair. There are more of you than of us."

"I ain't going over to the girls' side," Mark protested.

"We don't want any boys, anyway," Sarah shouted back.

Again Faith silenced them. "You don't want peace?"

"No!" Thomas tossed a snowball straight up and batted it down with his hand as if to prove his expertise.

"Forget it," Mark seconded.

"Then we have to make it a fair fight."

The boys were silent, apparently waiting for one of them to volunteer. No one did.

"I suggest that in order to even things up, the boys' side is restricted to the use of one hand. Agreed?"

The boys grinned and nodded.

"Your left hand," she added.

Their laughter and snickers quickly died out. "Ah, come on..."

Not giving the group a chance to argue, Faith tossed the first snowball, which landed just short of the snow fortification. Before the boys had time to react, she raced back to Sarah. The little girl was crouched behind the shelter and had accumulated a huge pile of snowballs.

Soon they were all laughing and pelting each other with snow. Faith managed to land several wildly thrown snowballs, but she was on the receiving end just as often. At one point she glanced toward the house and saw Charles looking out the living-room window.

Oh, no. Even a snowball fight was too much racket for him. Unfortunately, the distraction cost her. Thomas, who was fast becoming accustomed to pitching snowballs left-handed, scored a direct hit. The snowball struck her square in the chest. Snow sprayed up into her face, and Faith made a show of sputtering.

"Gotcha," Thomas cried and did a jig of triumph, leaping up and down with his arms above his head.

Faith glanced at the house again and saw Charles laughing. She did a double take. The man could actually laugh? This was news. Perhaps he wasn't so stuffy, after all. Perhaps she'd misread him entirely.

Was that possible?

Chapter Fifteen

"This is the Old North Church?" Emily stood outside Christ Church, made famous in the Longfellow poem. "The 'one if by land, two if by sea' church?"

"The very one," Ray assured her. "Boston's oldest surviving religious structure."

Emily tilted back her head and looked to the very top of the belfry. "If I remember my history correctly, a sexton…"

"Robert Newman."

She nodded. "He warned Paul Revere and the patriots that the British were coming."

"Correct. You may go to the head of the class."

Emily had always been fascinated by history. "I

loved school. I was a good student," she said. A trait her daughter had inherited.

"I can believe it," Ray said, guiding her inside the church.

They toured it briefly, and Emily marveled as Ray dramatically described that fateful night in America's history.

"How do you know so much about this?"

Ray grinned. "You mean other than through Charles, who's lived and breathed this stuff from the time he was a kid?"

"Yes."

"The truth is that, years ago, I edited a book—a mystery novel, actually—in which the Old North Church played a major role in the plot."

Emily was so enraptured by Boston's history that she'd forgotten Ray was an important figure in New York publishing.

"As a matter of fact, I have plenty of trivia in the back of my mind from my years as a hands-on editor."

As they walked, Ray described a number of books he'd edited and influential authors he'd worked with. Apparently he no longer did much of that. Instead he had a more administrative role.

Emily found it very easy to talk to Ray, and the hours melted away. It seemed they'd hardly left the condominium, but it was already growing dark. She admired the Christmas lights and festive displays, which weren't like those in Leavenworth, but equally appealing.

They stopped for a seafood dinner and then walked around some more, taking in the sights and sounds of the season. As Emily told him about Leavenworth, Ray grew more amused with each anecdote. "I wish I could be there to see Charles's reaction."

Emily continued to feel guilty about Ray's brother—and about Faith—but she couldn't have known. Her one wish was that Faith and Charles would be as compatible as she and Ray.

Being with him these last few days before Christmas made all the difference in the world. If not for Ray, she'd probably be holed up in the condo baking dozens of cookies and feeling sorry for herself.

"Despite all the mix-ups, I'm glad I'm here," she told him.

"I'm glad you're here, too," Ray said. "I'm enjoying your company so much. Do you want to know what else I'm enjoying?"

Emily could only guess. "Being in Boston again?"

"Well, that too. But what I mean is that I'm completely free of phone calls."

The first thing Ray had done, once he'd contacted

his office and informed his assistant that he wouldn't be returning until after the holidays, was turn off his cell phone.

"You might have missed an important call," she reminded him.

"Tough. Whoever's in the office can handle it this time. I'm unavailable." He laughed as he said it.

Emily laughed because he did, but from the little she'd learned about his work, it was a hectic series of meetings and continual phone calls. Ray must be under constant pressure, dealing with agents' and authors' demands, in addition to various vice-presidents, sales and marketing personnel, advertising firms and more. Although he held a prominent position with the company and obviously interacted with many people, he seemed as lonely as she was. He'd told her that aside from his work and a few social commitments, he had no reason to rush back to New York. Indeed, he seemed eager to stay here in Boston.

"Coffee?" he asked when they reached the Starbucks where she'd had her last encounter with Heather.

Emily hesitated, but then agreed. After all these hours of walking, she was exhausted and her feet hurt. Yet, at the same time, she was invigorated by everything she'd seen and done—and utterly charmed by Ray.

While he stepped up to the counter to order their drinks, she secured a table. As luck would have it, the only vacant one was the same table she'd occupied while waiting to meet her daughter. Her thoughts inevitably flashed to Heather, and Emily wondered where she was now and what she was doing. No, it was probably best not to know.

A few minutes later, Ray joined her with two tall cups of coffee. He slipped into the seat across from her. "Time like this is a luxury for me," he said.

"I want you to know how much I appreciate—"

He took her hand, stopping her. "What I'm trying to say, I guess, is that I've avoided it."

Emily frowned, uncertain she understood his meaning.

"I loved being with you today, talking and laughing with you. The truth is, I can't remember any day I've enjoyed more in a very long while."

"But I'm the one who's indebted to you."

"No," he said emphatically. "*I'm* the one who owes *you*. I'd forgotten," he said quietly, "what it's like to give myself a free day. To do something that's not related to work." He paused. "There seems to be a great deal in my life that I've let slide. I needed this wake-up call."

"In other words, I'm an alarm clock?"

He grinned. "You're more than that."

They were flirting with each other, she realized. Normally, conversations such as this terrified her. She'd married her high-school sweetheart and had rarely dated since Peter's death. Her daughter, sad as it was to admit, had more experience with men than she did.

Despite her determination not to, she was worrying about Heather again. Tears filled her eyes.

"Are you okay?"

Embarrassed, she nodded. Wiping the tears from her cheeks, she offered him a watery smile. "I was just thinking about my daughter."

"She's with friends, isn't she?"

"So she says." Emily rolled her eyes.

"Everyone has to grow up sooner or later, and among other things, that means learning how to judge other people's intentions." He shrugged. "Some lessons are more painful than others."

Sniffling a little, Emily agreed. "I can't think about Heather, otherwise I'll get upset. It's just that I had all these plans for the two of us over Christmas."

"What kind of plans?"

It seemed a little silly to tell Ray about them now. "I packed our favorite Christmas ornaments, so we could decorate a tree the same way we do every year."

"You and I could get a tree."

"You'd be willing to do that?"

"It's Christmas, isn't it? I haven't put up a tree in years."

"No tree?"

He chuckled. "Too much bother to do it on my own, but I'd love to help you. First thing in the morning, we'll buy a tree."

Her spirits brightened instantly.

"Anything else?"

"I always roast the traditional turkey, but I felt that since we were in Boston we should cook lobster. I love lobster tail with lots of melted butter. I've never prepared a whole lobster, though. I thought it'd be fun to go to a fish market and pick one out."

"That sounds like an excellent idea. Lobster for two."

"This is great!" Emily crowed happily.

After finishing their coffee, they walked back to the condominium hand in hand. By the time they rode up in the elevator, Ray had his arm around her. Being this close to him felt...natural. She rested her head against his shoulder.

Ray unlocked the door and swung it open, but he didn't immediately reach for the light switch. When Emily stepped into the living room, Ray turned her into his arms. He closed the front door with his foot, and they stood in near-darkness, the only light seeping in through the blinds. She leaned against him, eyes drifting shut.

Ray's palm cradled her cheek, his touch gentle. He rubbed his thumb across her lips and Emily sighed, wanting him to kiss her, afraid he wouldn't—yet afraid he would.

Standing on her toes, she slipped her arms around his neck and whispered, "Thank you for the most wonderful day."

"Thank *you*." His lips found hers then, and it was sweet and sensual all at once.

He brought her full against him as their mouths met again and again, one unhurried kiss following another. Emily's senses spun out of control but she pulled back, fearful of what might happen if they allowed this to continue.

Ray exhaled shakily. "I'm not sure that was a good idea, but I'm not sorry. Not at all…"

Emily kissed the side of his jaw. "Me, neither," she whispered.

She felt his smile. "Don't worry, Ray, I promise not to ravish you," she teased.

"Damn."

"Well…" Emily laughed softly. "I could reconsider."

It was Ray's turn to be amused. "You ready for the lights?"

"I suppose."

When Ray touched the switch, the room instantly went from dark to bright. But he didn't immediately release her.

When they separated and moved further into the room, Emily noticed the flashing message light on the phone. Ray noticed it, too. Emily's hopes soared—could it be Heather?—but then she remembered that her daughter didn't know where she was staying.

Ray pushed the caller ID button and groaned. "Four calls," he muttered, "and they're all from my mother."

Chapter Sixteen

Southern Florida in December was paradise. There was no other word for it. The beach was flawless, the water blue and clear and warm, the sunshine constant. It was as close to heaven as anyone who'd spent a winter in Boston could imagine.

What Heather didn't know was why she felt so miserable in such a perfect setting. She had every reason in the world to be happy, but she wasn't. To make matters worse, Elijah was growing irritated with her moods.

"Get me a beer," her hero called from where he was stretched out beneath a palm tree on the beach, one of his stalwart companions beside him.

Heather got up from the beach towel where she

was sunbathing and walked back into their motel room. She opened the small refrigerator and brought out a cold beer. Without a word she delivered it to Elijah. He looked at his friend, nodded, and the other man stood up and left.

"Let's talk," Elijah said, patting the sand next to him.

"About what?" Heather crossed her arms stubbornly.

"Sit down," he ordered. He pointed at the empty space his friend had just vacated.

Reluctantly Heather joined him.

"All right," he muttered after opening the beer. He took a long swig and wiped the back of his hand across his mouth. "What's wrong?"

"Nothing."

"Don't give me that. You haven't been yourself since we left Boston."

Heather didn't say anything. He knew she felt terrible about leaving her mother behind. If he couldn't figure it out, then she wasn't going to tell him.

"I thought you'd like Florida." Elijah made it sound like an accusation, as if he'd done everything humanly possible to provide for her happiness.

"What's not to like?"

Elijah nodded. "Exactly—so what's the problem?"

"You're right. I'm not happy."

He wrapped his arm around her neck, the cold beer bottle dangling between two fingers. "What is it, babe?"

Heather cringed at his use of the word *babe,* but she'd given up trying to convince Elijah to call her anything else. What particularly irritated her was that she suspected it was the term he used with all his girlfriends.

"If you must know, I'm worried about my mother."

Elijah tightened his grip around her neck by taking another healthy swig of beer. "I thought we already talked that out."

"We talked." He seemed to think it was a closed subject. Heather wished it was, but none of this was turning out the way she'd hoped. The motel was a dump, she was sick of fast food, the other women didn't like her, and...

"What is it now?"

She shook her head, letting her long hair swing. "Nothing."

"Don't give me that," he said again. "You've been in a piss-poor mood from the get-go." He spread his arms and looked out at the rolling waves of the ocean. "Here we are in paradise and you're whining about your mother." He made it sound ludicrous.

Maybe it was, but Heather couldn't help herself. "I'm just worried about her."

"You're *worried* about mommy?" Now he made it seem like one big joke and that infuriated her even more.

"You don't have a clue," Heather cried. Vaulting to her feet, she tore down the beach, kicking up sand. A few minutes later, she was out of breath and started walking, her eyes filled with tears.

"Wait up," Elijah shouted.

She was surprised he'd come after her. Heather waited for him and then fell into his arms, weeping softly. Elijah held her in his muscular embrace.

"All right, babe, tell me all about it."

"You don't understand."

He kissed the side of her neck. "I can't be happy when you're miserable, you know."

And that made Heather remember why she loved him. Taking a deep breath, she tried to explain.

"Mom was born and raised in this dinky town in Washington State. This is her first trip to the East Coast."

"Get out of here! Her first trip?"

Heather nodded. "I left her all by herself."

"She loves you, right?"

"Of course. She's my mother."

"And you love her?"

"Of course—why else would I feel so awful?"

"Don't you think she'd want you to be happy?" Elijah asked as if following his logic was a simple thing.

"Yes, I suppose, but…" Heather felt confused and unsure. "I wish it was that easy."

"It is," he argued. "Just don't think about her."

"She's probably miserable and alone, and I did this to her."

"Babe," he said, more gruffly this time. "You didn't ask her to fly to Boston, did you?" When she shook her head, he muttered, "Then get a grip. The others are starting to complain."

"Who?"

"Peaches, for one."

Heather had tried to make friends with the women but they were impossible. She was a college girl, so they disliked and mistrusted her on sight.

"Peaches would complain about me no matter what I said or did."

"That's not true," Elijah asserted.

"Yes, it is. It's the same with the others." She didn't mention the way the other girls had made fun of her. Heather wasn't accustomed to riding on a motorcycle for long periods of time and suffered a bad case of TB, better known as tired butt.

"Walk with me," Heather suggested, tugging at his arm.

Elijah hesitated. His only concession to the beach was a sleeveless T-shirt. Even in the Miami sunshine, he wore his leather pants and boots.

"Just for a little way," Heather coaxed.

Elijah glanced over his shoulder and then nodded. "Not far, all right?"

"Sure." At the moment Heather would have promised him anything. They hadn't been alone since they'd left Boston. Even the motel room was shared with another couple. Naturally she was stuck with Peaches, who made no effort to hide her disdain for Heather.

They walked for a while, until Elijah decided they'd gone far enough, and sat down in the sand. "Tell me about *your* mother," Heather said, pressing her head against his shoulder.

Elijah was silent for a moment. "Not much to tell. She's a regular mother, or I think she would've been if she'd stayed around."

"I'm sorry." Heather felt bad for bringing up unhappy memories.

"It was a bummer after she left, but I survived."

"What was Christmas like for you?"

Elijah pulled out his pack of cigarettes, lit one up and took a drag before responding. "It wasn't any Santa down the chimney, if that's what you mean."

"How so?"

"Did I mention my dad took off a year before my mother?"

"No." Heather felt worse than ever.

"No big deal. We had good foster parents, and the state always made sure we had at least one gift under the tree."

Heather slid her arm around his waist.

"What about you?" he asked.

"You don't want to know."

"Sure I do," he countered.

Heather wasn't sure where to start. "I told you about Leavenworth, right?"

"Yeah, it's a Bavarian kind of town, you said."

"Right. Christmas is a big deal there and with my mother, too. I think she always wanted to make up for the fact that my dad died when I was young, so she really did the Christmas thing up big. We had dozens of traditions." Heather grew sad again, just thinking about all she was missing.

"You're a big girl now," Elijah told her. "Traditions are for kids."

Heather nodded but she wanted to tell him that people didn't outgrow their need for a Christmas stocking or decorating a tree or hot apple cider on Christmas Eve.

Elijah sighed. "Are you okay now?"

She shrugged. "I guess."

"Good." He stabbed his cigarette into the sand and then stood. Extending his hand to her, Elijah helped Heather to her feet.

"Thank you," she whispered, kissing him.

"That's much better," he said. He placed one arm around her waist and drew her close. "Forget about your mother."

Heather doubted she could. Despite everything, she knew her mother was all alone in Boston, completely miserable without her.

Chapter Seventeen

Faith basted the roasting chicken and closed the oven door as quietly as possible. Rather than mash the potatoes with the mixer, she decided to use the hand utensil in an effort to cut down on noise. As far as she could discern, the cranky professor had enjoyed her cooking the night before. The stuffed green peppers had disappeared in short order.

By six, the house was dark and dreary. Faith went from room to room, drawing the curtains and turning on lights. She played solitaire for an hour. Then she finished the dinner preparations and set the table for one. Before serving herself, she sautéed the green beans with bacon bits and onion, sliced the gelatin salad and carved the roast chicken. Then she lit two candles on the dining-room table and filled her own plate from the dishes in the kitchen. The closed den door discouraged her from letting Charles know dinner was ready. Once she'd eaten, she'd make up a plate for him and leave it on the kitchen counter; he could warm it up in the microwave when he was hungry. That was what she'd done yesterday.

Faith sat down at the far end of the dining-room table and spread the linen napkin across her lap. Emily always used real cloth napkins. Faith admired that about her friend. Living on her own, Faith tended to treat meals as a necessary evil, but when she dined with Emily, meals were an event to be savored and shared. So, in Emily's house and in Emily's honor, Faith would keep up this tradition.

Reaching for the merlot she'd bought that day, she started to pour herself a glass, then stopped, the bottle suspended, when she realized Charles had emerged from the den. He stood in the dining room, looking a bit disoriented. He stared at her as if he'd forgotten she was in the house.

Faith stood. "Would you like me to get you a plate?"

Charles frowned at the grandfather clock. "I had no idea it was six-thirty." The clock marked the half hour with a resounding clang, punctuating his words. "Uh, do you mind if I join you?" he asked.

Faith was too shocked to reply. "P-please do," she stuttered after an embarrassingly long pause.

Charles went into the kitchen for a plate and served himself from the various dishes she'd prepared, then returned to the dining room. He sat at the opposite end of the table.

They remained awkward with each other. He made a polite comment about the food; she responded with equal politeness.

Silence! Faith desperately wished she had the nerve to put on a Christmas CD—maybe a Celtic Christmas recording Emily had. Or an instrumental of classic carols.

She cleared her throat. "Would you like some merlot?" she offered. She preferred red wine to white, which was why she chose to drink a red with chicken.

"Thank you."

Before she could stand, he got up and retrieved a second wineglass from the kitchen, poured his wine and sat down.

An uneasy silence settled between them once again. Faith picked up her fork and resumed eating.

"How did your snow war end yesterday afternoon?" Charles asked in a casual voice.

"Successfully—for the girls," Faith told him in cordial tones. "The boys surrendered when they saw they were outwitted and overpowered by us."

Charles nodded. "I had a feeling the boy-team needed my assistance."

This time, Faith managed to hide her shock.

He glanced at her and grinned—actually grinned. "My aim is excellent, if I do say so myself."

"Oh." She couldn't think of a thing to say. What suddenly filled her mind was a vision of Charles Brewster throwing snowballs, surrounded by a swarm of young boys.

"So you survived the adventure unscathed."

"I sure did." She wasn't telling him how much her shoulders ached and she'd ended up taking aspirin before retiring last night, nor did she mention that she'd soaked in a hot tub for twenty minutes. Today she'd gone shopping, list in hand, and when she returned, she'd lounged in front of the fireplace with a good book and a cup of warm cocoa, keeping as still as possible.

"You enjoyed seeing me get plowed, didn't you?" she asked, again in the most conversational of tones.

"Dare I admit that I did?" He smiled once more, and it transformed his face, reminding Faith of her reaction to his laughter the day before. *Had* she been wrong about him?

"I wish you had joined us," she told him impulsively.

"I was tempted."

"Why didn't you?"

He shrugged and lifted his wineglass. "Mainly because I've got work to do—but that isn't the only reason I'm here." He gestured at the window. "Hard as it is to believe, I came here to avoid Christmas."

Had her mouth been full, Faith would have choked. "You came to *Leavenworth* to avoid Christmas?"

He shrugged again. "I thought it would be a nice quiet prison community."

"That's Leavenworth, Kansas."

"I eventually remembered that."

Faith couldn't keep from laughing.

"I'm delighted you find this so amusing."

"Sorry, I don't mean to make fun of your situation, but it really is kind of funny."

"It's your situation, too," he said. "You're stuck here, just like I am."

Faith didn't need any reminders. "What are you working on?" she asked in an effort to change the subject.

"I'm a history professor at Harvard, specializing in the early-American era."

It made sense that he taught at Harvard, Faith supposed; he lived in Boston, after all.

"I'm contracted to write a textbook, which is due at my publisher's early in the new year."

"How far are you with it?"

"Actually it's finished. I was almost done when I

arrived, and my goal is to polish the rough draft in the remaining time I'm here."

"Will you be able to do that?"

"I'm astonished at all the writing I've accomplished since I got here. I finished the rough draft about fifteen minutes ago." He couldn't quite suppress a proud smile.

"Then congratulations are in order," she said, raising her wineglass to salute him.

Charles raised his glass, too, and they simultaneously sipped the merlot.

"Actually, early American history is a favorite subject of mine," Faith told him. "I teach English literature at the junior high level but I include some background in American history whenever I can. Like when I teach Washington Irving. The kids love 'The Legend of Sleepy Hollow.'"

"Don't we all?"

After that, they launched into a lively discussion, touching on the Boston Tea Party, Longfellow's poetry, writings of the Revolutionary War period and the War of 1812.

"You know your history," he said. "And your American literature."

"Thank you." She heard the admiration in his voice and it warmed her from the inside out. "I like to think I can hold my own in snowball fights and battles of wits and words."

"No doubt you can." Charles stood and carried both plates into the kitchen. "Shall we finish our wine in the living room?" he surprised her by asking.

"That would be lovely."

The fire had died down to embers, so Charles added another log. He sat in the big overstuffed chair and stretched out his long legs, crossing them at the ankle. Faith sat on the rug by the fireplace, bringing her knees up to her chin as she reveled in the warmth.

"I've always loved this town," she said.

"Thus far, I haven't been very impressed," Charles said, a little sardonically. "But my predicament hasn't turned out to be nearly as disastrous as I feared."

Faith couldn't have held back a smile if she tried. "I don't think I'll ever forget the look on your face when I showed up with Santa and the elves."

"I don't think I'll ever forget the look on yours when I walked out of that bathroom."

"I was expecting Emily."

"I wasn't expecting anyone."

They both laughed.

"You're not nearly so intimidating when you laugh."

"Me, intimidating?" Charles asked as if she were joking.

"You can be, you know."

He seemed puzzled by that, shaking his head.

"I suspect you don't get angry often," she went on, "but when you do…"

"When I do," he said, completing her thought, "people know it."

He'd certainly made his feelings known shortly after her arrival. "I really appreciate your letting me stay," she told him.

"Actually, after a meal like that and last night's too, I think I'm the fortunate one."

"I've enjoyed cooking the last couple of days. I don't do much of it anymore. Usually I grab something on my way home from school."

"Me, too," he said. "You live alone?"

Faith nodded. "I've been divorced for more than five years." She was too embarrassed to admit how short-lived her marriage had been. "What about you?"

"I've never been married."

"Are you involved with anyone?" Faith asked the question before she had time to think about what it might reveal.

Charles shook his head. "No, my work's always been my life."

Suddenly the room seemed to grow very warm. Faith looked up and found Charles studying her as if seeing her for the first time.

Uncomfortable under his scrutiny, Faith came gracefully to her feet. "I'd better do the dishes," she said.

"Wait." Charles stood, too. "I'll help."

"No, really, that isn't necessary." Faith didn't understand *why* it was so important to put distance between them, but it was. She knew that instinctively. They'd shared a wonderful meal, found common ground, discussed history and even exchanged a few personal facts. They were attracted to each other. She felt it; he felt it, too, Faith was sure, and it unnerved her.

"Okay," Charles said. He stood no more than a foot away from her.

The tension between them seemed to throb like a living thing. It took Faith a moment to realize that Charles was responding to her statement about not needing help with the dishes.

She started to walk away, abandoning her wine, when he caught her hand. She stood frozen, half facing the kitchen, her fingers lightly held in his. She sensed that if she turned back, he'd probably kiss her. He'd given her the choice.

Slowly, almost against her will, Faith turned. Charles drew her into the circle of his arms and brought his mouth down on hers.

The kiss was wonderful. They strained against each other, wanting, needing to give more, receive more, *feel* more.

When it was over, they stared at each other as if equally perplexed.

"Wow," Faith mumbled.

"You're telling me!"

Charles pulled her back into his embrace and held her tightly. "I'm ready to be wowed again. How about you?"

Faith's heart fluttered with excitement. This was the best surprise yet, she mused, as she closed her eyes and tilted her mouth toward his.

Chapter Eighteen

Emily had the bacon sizzling and muffins baking by the time Ray came out of his brother's bedroom. His hair was still wet from the shower, and he wore a fresh set of clothes. Emily assumed they'd come out of Charles's closet, because Ray hadn't brought a suitcase. Apparently the two brothers were close enough in size for Ray to wear his brother's clothes.

"Good morning," she greeted him cheerfully.

Ray muttered something indistinguishable and stumbled over to the coffeepot. He poured himself a mug. "Are you always this happy in the morning?" he asked, after his first restorative sip.

"Always," Emily said, just as cheerfully as before.

Ray stared at her. "I've heard there are two kinds

of people in the world. Those who wake up and say 'Good Morning, God' and those who say 'Good God, morning.'"

Emily laughed. "You don't need to tell me which one you are."

"Or you." He settled on the stool by the counter, propped up his elbows and slowly sipped his coffee. When he'd finished his first cup, he was smiling again and eager for breakfast.

Emily set their plates on the counter and joined him, bringing the coffeepot for refills.

"Are you still interested in getting a Christmas tree?" she asked, as Ray dug into his bacon and eggs.

"Definitely, but first I think I'd better call my mother."

They'd listened to the messages the night before. Bernice Brewster made it sound imperative that she speak to her oldest son *immediately*.

After breakfast, Ray went to retrieve the portable phone.

"It's barely six in Arizona," she warned.

"Mom's an early riser and trust me—she's waiting with bated breath to hear from me."

He knew his mother well, because almost as soon as he'd dialed, Bernice was on the line. While they exchanged greetings, Emily scraped off the plates and set them in the dishwasher. She could only hear one end of the conversation, but Ray seemed to have trouble getting a word in edgewise. After a while, he placed the receiver carefully on the counter and walked away. He leaned against one of the stools, arms crossed, and waited patiently for his mother to finish her tirade. Even from the other side of the kitchen, Emily could hear the woman ranting.

"Ray," she whispered, half amused and half shocked at what he'd done.

He poured himself a third mug of coffee and shrugged elaborately.

After a few minutes, he lifted the receiver and pretended to be outraged. "Yes, Mother. Yes, of course, it's *dreadful.*" He rolled his eyes. "What do I plan to do about it? Frankly, nothing. Charles is over twenty-one and for that matter, so am I. Have a wonderful Christmas—your gift should arrive by the 24th. I'll be in touch. Bye now." He listened a few seconds more and then turned off the phone.

"Did you, uh, reassure your mother?" Emily asked.

"I doubt it." Ray chuckled. "She wanted to know what's going on with Charles. I didn't tell her, because basically I don't know. Besides, hard though it is for my mother to grasp, it's none of her business who Charles is with."

Still, Emily understood the other woman's concerns. "She's worried that both her sons are with strange women." She gave a short laugh. "Not *strange*, but strangers."

He smiled, too. "You know, frankly I think she'd be overjoyed if she met you. You're exactly the kind of woman she's wanted to introduce me to all these years."

Emily wasn't sure what to make of his comment. "Is that good or bad?"

"Good," he assured her and briefly touched her cheek. "Very good."

As soon as they'd cleaned up the kitchen, they put on their winter coats and ventured outside. The sky was dull gray, threatening snow. Arms linked, they walked several blocks until they found a Christmas tree lot.

"Merry Christmas." The lot attendant, a college student from the look of him, wandered over when they entered. He didn't seem especially busy, Emily noticed, but with only three days until Christmas most people had their trees up and decorated.

"Hello," Emily said, distracted by Ray who was straightening a scraggly fir that leaned against the makeshift wire fence. She shook her head at the pathetic little tree with its broken limbs and one bald side.

"Do you want your tree tall or small?" the young man asked. His breath made foggy wisps in the air.

"Medium-sized," Emily said.

He stared at her with narrowed eyes. "Would you mind telling me where you got that scarf?"

Emily turned away from the Christmas trees to look at the young man. "I knit it. Why?"

He shrugged. "I had a friend who had a similar one. That's all."

A chill raced down Emily's spine. "Your friend wouldn't happen to be Heather Springer, would she?"

"Yeah," he said excitedly. "How'd you know?"

"She's my daughter."

"You're Heather's mother?" He whipped off his glove and thrust out his hand. "I'm Ben Miller," he told her. "Heather and I were in Art History together."

Ben Miller…Ben Miller… She had it! "Didn't you and Heather date for a while?"

"Yeah." He replaced his glove and rubbed his hands together. "I apparently wasn't…dangerous enough for her."

"Dangerous?"

"Never mind," Ben shook his head. "She's seeing Elijah now. Elijah with no last name." He spit out the words. "From what I hear, she's headed down to Florida with him and a bunch of his no-account friends."

The urge to defend Heather rose quickly, but died within the space of a single heartbeat. Emily could tell that he'd been hurt by Heather's actions—just as she herself had been. "Heather'll be back soon, I'm sure," she murmured. It was the best she could do.

"You came out to spend Christmas with her and she left anyway?" Ben sounded thoroughly disgusted.

"Yes…"

"You know, when Heather told me her plans for Christmas, I assumed it wouldn't take her long to see that she's making a mistake."

Emily'd hoped so, too.

"But if she could turn her back on her own mother at Christmas, then she isn't the person I thought she was." Ben's eyes hardened. "To tell you the truth, I don't care if I ever see her again." He walked over to another section of the lot. "There are a couple of nice trees over here," he said, all business now.

Emily and Ray followed him.

"Give her time," Emily said, squeezing his forearm with one mittened hand.

Ben glanced at her. "She isn't interested in me anymore."

Emily hung her head, fearing her daughter hadn't given her a single thought, either.

Sensing her mood, Ray placed his hand on Emily's shoulder. "You okay?" he asked.

She nodded. Nothing she said or did now would make a difference to what Heather had done or how

Emily felt about it. But Ben seemed like a decent, hardworking young man and she felt bad that her daughter had so obviously hurt him.

"With Christmas this close, we don't have much to choose from," Ben apologized. He picked through several trees, then chose a tall, full one. "This is probably a little bigger than you wanted, but it's the best I've got."

Ray looked skeptical and circled the tree. "What do you think?" he asked Emily.

"It's perfect." She winked at Ben.

"We'll take it," Ray said and reached for his wallet.

Without a car they were forced to carry the tree back to the condominium. They walked in single file, Ray holding the trunk in one hand and a stand in the other, and Emily behind him, supporting the treetop. They must've been something of a spectacle, because they got lots of stares along the way.

Once inside the condo, they saw the message light blinking again. Ray checked the caller ID and groaned. "It's my mother. Again."

"Are you going to call her back?"

"Of course, but not anytime soon."

Emily smiled. While Ray fit the tree in the stand, she took out the decorations she'd brought from Seattle.

"You got all that in a single suitcase?" Ray marveled when she spread everything out.

"Two very large suitcases if you must know. Don't forget the stuff already on the mantel."

He shook his head, but Emily could tell he was enjoying this.

The living room was compact, and after a long debate, they decided the best place for the tree was by the window, although that entailed moving the furniture around.

"It's beautiful," Emily told him. She handed him the first decoration—a felt snowman complete with knitted scarf. "I made that for Heather the year she was in kindergarten," Emily explained.

Ray placed it on a tree limb and picked up a second ornament. "Does every one of these have some significance?"

Emily nodded. "Each and every one."

"That's wonderful."

She was surprised he'd appreciate her sentimentality. "You don't think I'm silly to treasure these ornaments?"

"Not at all. You've given your daughter a lovely tradition."

At the mention of Heather, Emily bit her lip, overwhelmed by sadness.

Ray wrapped his arms around her. "My guess is she's got just enough freedom to be miserable," he said softly.

Emily doubted it, but she was grateful for his encouragement.

"Everything's going to work out for the best," he assured her. "Just wait and see."

Emily hoped he was right.

Chapter Nineteen

Faith woke up to the sound of Charles rummaging around in the kitchen. Grabbing her housecoat, she hurried down the stairs.

"Morning," he said, grinning sheepishly. "I hope I didn't wake you."

Faith rubbed the sleep from her eyes. He had to be joking. But then she glanced at the kitchen clock and couldn't believe she'd slept this late. It was the deepest, most relaxed sleep she'd had in months. She hadn't realized how tired she'd been.

"Coffee?" Charles lifted the glass pot.

"Please." She tightened the belt of her velour robe and sat down at the table, shaking the hair away from her face. Charles brought her a mug, which he'd filled with coffee. She added cream and held it in both hands, basking in the warmth that spread through her palms. They'd spent the most enjoyable evening talking and drinking wine and...

"What are your plans for today?" he asked.

Faith hadn't given it much consideration. "Maybe I'll walk into town a bit later."

Charles mulled that over. "Would you object to company?"

"You?" she gasped.

He shrugged in a self-conscious manner. "Unless you'd rather I didn't come with you."

"But I—what about your work?" Naturally she'd enjoy his company but Charles had insisted he was in Leavenworth to work and didn't want to be distracted from his purpose.

"I was up early this morning and got quite a bit done."

"Oh."

"I felt I should leave the project for a while, now that the rough draft is done. I'd like to give my mind a rest."

"Oh." All at once Faith seemed incapable of words consisting of more than one syllable.

"So—it seems I have the luxury of some free time."

"Oh." She sipped her coffee. "But I thought you hated Christmas?"

"I do. For...various reasons. It's far too commercial. The true meaning's been lost in all the frenzy of the season."

"Christmas is what each one of us makes it," Faith felt obliged to tell him.

"Exactly."

Faith swallowed. "I was going into town to do some shopping. Uh, Christmas shopping," she added. She met his eyes as she looked for some indication that he'd be interested in accompanying her. Men were notoriously impatient when it came to browsing through stores. And an avowed Christmas-hater...

He didn't say anything for a moment, then set his mug aside. "I see. Well, in that case, I've got other projects I can work on."

"Oh." She couldn't disguise her disappointment.

Charles frowned. "*Would* you like my company?"

"Very much," she said quickly.

"Then I read you wrong."

"I'm just afraid it wouldn't interest you," she explained.

"I'd enjoy being out in the fresh air. I'll get my coat." He was like a kid eager to start a promised adventure.

"Whoa." Faith raised one hand. "Give me time. I've got to shower and dress, and I wouldn't mind a little something to eat first."

"Okay." He seemed amenable enough to that.

Faith wasn't quite sure what had prompted the change in him, but she wasn't complaining. She poured cereal and milk into a bowl, and ate every bite. Drinking the last of her coffee, she hurried back up the stairs and grabbed her jeans, a sweater and fresh underwear. She showered, dressed and dried her hair. When she came out of the bathroom, she found her boots, put them on and laced them up.

"Charles?" He didn't seem to be anywhere around. "Charles," she called, more loudly this time.

By chance she happened to glance out the window—to discover him surrounded by half a dozen neighborhood boys and Sarah. The children were apparently trying to talk him into something, but Charles clearly wasn't interested. Several times he shook his head and gestured dismissively with his gloved hands.

Faith threw on her coat and dashed out of the house, fastening her buttons as she went. She could see that Charles had begun to sweep the snow off the porch steps and had apparently been interrupted in his task by the children.

"Hi, Faith," Thomas called out. "You want to go sledding with us?"

"Ah…" She looked to Charles for some indication of his feelings. "What about you?"

Charles shook his head. "The last time I was on a sled, I was thirteen years old and too young to know better."

"It's fun," Thomas Kennedy promised.

"Go down the hill just once and you'll see what we mean." Mark's young voice was filled with excitement.

"You just gotta," Sarah insisted, tugging at Charles's hand.

Several of the older kids had lost interest in persuading Charles; they were already across the street, pulling their sleds.

"Come on," Faith said. "You need to do this or you'll lose face with the kids."

"Faith, I'm not sure it's a good idea."

"It'll be fun. You'll see."

"Faith, listen, I'm not entirely comfortable with this."

"They'll pester you until you give in, you realize?"

Charles seemed to need more convincing. "I'll go first," she told him. "Just do what I do, and you won't have a problem."

"People can get killed sledding," he mumbled to no one in particular.

She looked both ways before crossing the street. "People get killed on their way to work, too."

"This isn't encouraging."

"I'll go first," she said again.

"No," he countered as they trudged up the hill. "If this has to be done, I'll do it."

Thomas proudly showed Charles how to lie flat on the sled and how to steer with his arms. Charles still seemed unsure, but he was enough of a sport to lie prone, his feet hanging over the sled. He looked up at Faith with an expression that said if he died, it would be her fault.

"Are your life insurance premiums paid up?" she teased.

"Very funny," he grumbled.

Faith laughed, but her amusement soon turned to squeals of concern as the sled started down the snowy hill. Because of his weight, Charles flew downward at breakneck speed. His momentum carried him much farther than the children and straight toward the playground equipment.

"Turn!" she screamed. "Charles, turn the sled!" He couldn't hear her, so she did the only thing she could—and that was run after him. She stumbled and fell any number of times as she vaulted down the hill. Before long, she was on her backside, sliding down the snow and slush with only the thin protection of her jeans. The icy cold seeped through her clothes, but she didn't care. If anything happened to him, she'd never forgive herself.

Charles disappeared under the swing set and continued on for several feet before coming to a stop just short of the frozen pond.

"Charles, Charles!" Faith raced after him, oblivious now to her wet bottom and the melting snow running down her calves.

Charles leaped off the sled. His smile stretched from ear to ear as he turned toward her. "That was *incredible!*"

"You were supposed to stop," she cried, furious with him and not afraid to let him know it.

"Then you should have said so." He was by far the calmer one.

"You could've been hurt!"

"Yes, I know, but weren't you the one who said I could just as easily die on my way to work?"

"You're an idiot!" She hurled herself into his arms, nearly choking him. She felt like bursting into tears of relief that he was safe and unhurt.

Charles clasped her around the waist and lifted her off the ground. "Hey, hey, I'm fine."

"I know...I know—but I expected you to stop where the kids do."

"I will next time."

"Next time?"

"Come on," he said, and set her down. "It's your turn."

"No, thanks." Faith raised both her hands and took

a step backward. "I already had a turn. I went down the hill on my butt, chasing after you."

He laughed, and the sound was pure magic. He kissed her cold face. "Go change clothes. As soon as you're ready we'll go into town."

"Are you staying in the park?"

Charles nodded. "Of course. A man's got to do what a man's got to do."

Shaking her head, she sighed. What on earth had she created here? One ride down the hill, and Charles Brewster was a thirteen-year-old boy all over again.

Chapter Twenty

Heather could hardly hear a thing over all the noise in the Hog's Breath Tavern in Key West, Florida. Peaches was eyeing Elijah with the voluptuous look of a woman on the prowl. Heather gazed across the room rather than allow herself to be subjected to such blatant attempts to lure Elijah away.

Slipping off the bar stool, she squeezed past crowded tables in a search for the ladies' room. This entire vacation wasn't anything like she'd imagined. She'd pictured sitting with Elijah on a balmy beach, singing Christmas carols and holding each other close. His idea of fun was riding twelve hours a day on his Harley with infrequent breaks, grabbing stale sandwiches in a mini-mart, and drinking beer with people who disliked and distrusted her.

Inside the rest room, Heather waited in line for a stall. Once she was hidden by the privacy of the cubicle, she buried her face in her hands. It was time to admit she'd made a mistake—hard as that was on her pride—but she'd had about as much as she could take of Elijah and his so-called friends.

When she left the ladies' room, Elijah was back at the bar with a fresh beer, which he raised high in the air when he saw her, evidently to tell her where he was. As if she hadn't figured it out by now. If Elijah didn't have a beer in his hand, then he was generally with a woman and most of the time it wasn't her.

"Babe," he said, draping his arm around her neck. "Where'd you go?"

"To the powder room."

He slobbered a kiss on the corner of her mouth. "Want another beer?"

"No, thanks."

"Hey, this is a party."

Maybe—but she wasn't having any fun. "So it seems."

His smile died and a flash of anger showed in his eyes. "What's your problem?"

Frankly, at this point there were too many to list. "Can we talk?" she asked.

"Now?" He glanced irritably around.

"Please."

"Sure, whatever." Frowning, he slid off the stool. With his arm still around her neck, he led the way outside. "You don't like Key West?" he asked as soon as they were outside. His tone suggested that anyone who couldn't have a good time in this town was in sad shape.

"What's not to like?" This had become her standard response. And she did like Key West. But the things she wanted to do—take history walks, visit Hemingway House, check out bookstores—were of no interest to the others.

"Well, then?" Elijah took another swallow of beer and pitched the bottle into a nearby trash can. "You've been in a sour mood ever since we got here."

"Maybe I don't like you clinging to Peaches."

His laugh was short and abrupt. "You're jealous. Damn, I should've figured as much."

"Not really." She hadn't fully analyzed her feelings. The only emotion she'd experienced watching the two of them had been disgust. That, and sadness at her own misguided choices.

"So what's the big deal?" he demanded.

"There isn't one."

They stopped walking and faced each other. Elijah crossed his arms, leaning against his motorcycle as the din of raised voices and loud music spilled out from the Hog's Breath. Elijah looked longingly over his shoulder, as if he resented being dragged away from all the fun. The partyers continued their revelry, apparently not missing either of them.

"Dammit, tell me what you want."

His impatience rang in her ears. "What are your— our plans for Christmas Day?"

"Christmas Day?" Elijah said. He seemed confused by the question. "What do you mean?"

"You know, December twenty-fifth? Two days from now? What are we going to do to celebrate Christmas?"

He looked at her, his eyes blank. "I haven't thought that far ahead. Why?"

"Why?" she repeated. "Because it's important to me."

He considered this. "What would you like to do?"

Her throat clogged with emotion as she remembered the way she'd celebrated Christmas with her mother, all the special traditions that had marked her childhood. She hadn't realized how much she'd miss those or how empty the holidays would feel without her family.

"I was hoping," Heather said, being as forthright and honest as she could, "that we'd find a small palm tree on the beach and decorate it like a real Christmas tree."

This seemed to utterly baffle Elijah. "Decorate it with what? Toilet paper?"

"I…don't know. Something. Maybe we could find sea shells and string those and cut out paper stars."

Elijah shrugged. "Would that make you happy?"

"I…I don't know. I dreamed of sitting in the sand with you and looking up at the night sky, singing Christmas carols."

Elijah rubbed his hand over his face. "I don't sing, and even if I did, I don't know the words to any of those carols. Well, maybe the one about the snowman. What the hell was his name again? Frisky?"

"Frosty."

"Yeah, Frosty."

"But you can hum, can't you?" Heather had a fairly decent voice. It didn't matter if he sang or not; all that mattered was being together and in love and sharing something important. Maybe creating a new tradition of their own…

"Heather, listen," Elijah said as he unfolded his arms and slowly straightened. "I'm not the kind of guy who decorates palm trees with paper stars or sings about melting snowmen."

"But I thought—"

"What?" He slapped his hand against the side of his head in frustration. "*What* were you thinking?"

"I like to party, too, but a steady diet of it grows old after a while."

"Says who?"

"Me," she cried. She'd never asked Elijah where he got his money, but she was beginning to think she should. "You didn't even consult me about having all these other people along."

"Hey," Elijah snapped, thrusting up both palms in a gesture of surrender. "You didn't *consult* me about all this Christmas junk you're so keen on, either."

He was right, but his sarcasm didn't make her feel any better. "I thought it would be just the two of us."

"Well, it isn't. I've got friends, and I'm not letting any woman get between me and my people."

"Your…people?"

"You know what I mean."

Unfortunately, Heather was beginning to understand all too well.

"Peaches warned me about college girls," he muttered.

"Ben warned me about you," she returned.

"Who the hell is Ben?"

"A friend." Heather wanted to kick herself for not listening, but it was too late for that.

"College girls are nothing but trouble."

"You didn't used to think that," Heather reminded him. "Not about me." From the moment they met, he'd said he didn't want to get involved with a college girl, and she'd taken that as a challenge to change his mind. She'd wanted to prove…what? She didn't know. Possibly how incredibly foolish she could be.

"I didn't used to think about a lot of things," Elijah said emphatically. "I've got a weakness for good girls, but the first thing they want to do is change me. Thing is, I'm content just the way I am. I'm not ever going to sit under any Christmas tree and sing silly songs. The sooner you accept that, the better."

Heather looked down the road and nodded. "I'm never going to be happy living like this." Her wide gesture took in the bar, the motorcycles, a group of hysterically laughing people clambering out of a cab.

"Like what?"

"Like this," she said. "Life is more than one big party, you know?"

"No, I don't," he countered.

"Fine." It wouldn't do any good to argue. "I'm leaving."

"You won't get any argument from me, but I'm not taking you to Boston, if that's what you want."

"No." She'd never ask that of him. "I'll catch a bus to Miami in the morning and fly back."

"What about money?" he asked, and the way he said it made it clear she was on her own.

"I'll be fine."

Elijah snorted. "Mommy's credit card to the rescue, right?"

Heather did have an emergency credit card her mother had given her, and she'd be forced to use it. In three years, she'd never had reason to do so, but she did now. Still, she was determined to pay back every last penny.

"Yes, Mommy's credit card. I'm fortunate to have a mother."

Elijah considered that for a moment, then nodded in agreement. "That's probably the reason you're in college. You had parents who gave a damn about you."

"I'm sorry it didn't work out for us," she told Elijah, sad now.

He shrugged casually. "Don't worry about it. We had a few good times."

"No hard feelings?"

Elijah shook his head. "You'll be all right, and so will I."

Heather knew that what he said was true. She should also have known, when she left Boston, that this arrangement would never work. Now she had two days to get back there and find her mother. Her poor, desperate mother in a strange town, without any friends…

Chapter Twenty-One

The phone rang as Ray and Emily sat by the Christmas tree, both cross-legged, sipping wine and listening to a Christmas concert on the radio.

"Don't answer that," he warned. "It might be my mother."

Emily smiled and hopped up to check Caller ID. "It's my phone number back in Washington," she said, picking up the receiver. "Hello?"

"Emily? It's Faith."

"Oh, Faith," Emily said, instantly cheered. "It's so good to hear from you."

"Is everything all right?" her friend asked.

"Everything is positively wonderful." Emily looked over to where Ray sat with his wineglass.

"It is here, too," Faith confessed.

"What about Charles?" Emily was sure she hadn't heard her friend correctly. Faith actually sounded happy, but that couldn't be possible, since she was stuck with a Christmas-hating curmudgeon.

"Oh, Emily, Charles has been just *great*. He wasn't in the beginning, but then I realized he's just like everyone else, only a little more intense."

"Really?"

"Yes. In fact, this morning he went sledding with the Kennedy kids. Thomas talked him into it. He was reluctant at first, but once he got started there was no stopping him."

"Charles?" Although they'd never met, Emily had heard enough about Ray's brother to find this bit of news truly astonishing.

"Then Charles and I walked downtown and browsed the stores and he bought the cutest little birdhouse for your yard. It's got a snowy roof and a bright-red cardinal on top."

"*Charles* did that?"

"Yes, and then we had a fabulous lunch. He's working now, or at least that's what he said he was doing, but I think he's taking a nap."

Emily smiled. This definitely wasn't the man Ray had described. From everything he'd told her, Charles was the classic absentminded professor, as stuffy and staid as they come. And he hated Christmas. Something—or someone—had turned his world upside down, and Emily had a very good idea who that might be.

"Faith," Emily murmured, "are you interested in Charles? As a man?"

Her friend didn't answer right away. "Define interested."

"Romantically inclined."

That caught Ray's notice; he stood and walked over to the phone, sitting down on a nearby stool.

"I don't know." Faith's answer revealed her indecision. "Well, maybe." She sounded uncertain, as if she was surprised by her feelings and a little troubled. This relationship must be developing very quickly; Emily could identify with that.

"I think it's wonderful that the two of you are getting along so well."

"He's not at all the way he first seemed," Faith told her. "First impressions can be deceptive, don't you think?"

"Of course."

"But I didn't phone to talk about myself." Faith seemed even more flustered now. "I just wanted to see how you're doing."

Emily's gaze drifted to Ray. "Like I said, this is turning out to be a wonderful Christmas."

Her announcement was followed by a short pause. "Charles's brother is still there?"

"Yes." Emily didn't elaborate.

"So the two of you are hitting it off?"

"We are. We're getting along really well."

As if to prove how well, Ray came to stand behind Emily. He slipped his arms around her waist and kissed the back of her neck. Tiny shivers of delight danced down her spine and she closed her eyes, savoring his warmth and attention.

"Have you heard from Heather?" Faith asked.

Emily's eyes flew open. "Not a peep, but I don't expect to since she doesn't have this phone number."

"I guess she'll call after Christmas," Faith said.

Emily managed a few words of assent, then changed the subject. "It was so sweet of you to come to Leavenworth for Christmas. I just wish you'd let me know."

"And ruin the surprise?" Faith teased.

"Just like I surprised Heather."

Faith laughed softly. "I'll check in with you later. Bye for now."

"Okay. Talk to you soon." Emily hung up the phone and sighed as she turned to Ray to explain the call. "As you could tell, that was Faith."

"What's all this about my brother?"

He released her and Emily leaned against the

kitchen counter. "Charles apparently spent the morning sledding with the neighborhood kids."

Ray shook his head, frowning. "That's impossible. Not Charles. He'd never knowingly choose to be around kids."

"That's not all. After sledding, the two of them went Christmas shopping—and he bought me a gift. A birdhouse."

Ray's frown grew puzzled. "This is a joke, right?"

"Not according to Faith."

"Charles? My *brother,* Charles?"

"The very same. Apparently she tired him out, because he's napping."

"I've got to meet this friend of yours. She must be a miracle worker." He paused. "You're sure about all this?"

"That's what Faith told me, and I've never known her to exaggerate."

"Something must've happened to my brother. Maybe I should call him myself."

"Don't you think this is a good thing?" Emily asked. "Judging by everything you've said, your brother seems to have a single focus. His work. He wanted to escape Christmas and finish his book."

Ray nodded, but his expression had started to relax. "It's interesting when you put it that way," he said thoughtfully.

"How so?"

"It sounds as if you're describing me."

This surprised Emily. From the beginning, she'd viewed Charles as an introvert, in contrast to Ray, who was personable and outgoing.

"For years now, Christmas has meant nothing but a few extra days off. Every year, I send the obligatory gift to my mother—usually the latest big mystery and maybe a new coffee-table book with lots of scenic pictures. I attend a few parties, have my assistant mail out greeting cards, make a restaurant reservation for the twenty-fifth. But I haven't felt any real spirit until today. With you."

Emily's heart warmed at his words.

"I never go for even an hour without thinking about work or publishing. We've spent the entire day together, and I haven't once missed hearing my cell ring."

Emily had no idea their Christmas-tree adventure had meant so much to him. He'd seemed eager to hear about her homemade decorations and the traditions she had with her daughter. Later she'd felt a bit silly to be talking so much and certain she'd bored him with her endless stories. She was glad she hadn't.

Ray looked away as if he'd said more than he intended. "Are you ready for dinner? What about that Mexican place we passed?"

"I'm starving." Mexican food sounded divine and the perfect ending to a perfect day.

"Me, too. That's what you get for walking my feet off this afternoon," he said. "Now you have to feed me."

After they'd finished putting the final touches on the tree, they'd gone out for a light lunch of pizza and salad, then walked and walked. They'd had no real destination, but enjoyed being out of doors. They'd talked incessantly and Emily was surprised they had so much to discuss. She was a voracious reader and Ray questioned her about her favorite books and authors. Emily had questions of her own about the publishing industry, which fascinated her. She noticed, though, that neither of them talked much about their private lives. Their conversations skirted around their thoughts and feelings, but the more time they spent together, the more they revealed.

Chapter Twenty-Two

Faith replaced the telephone receiver, and a happy feeling spread through her. What had felt like a disaster a few days earlier now seemed to be working wonderfully well—for her *and* her dearest friend.

As if her thoughts had awakened him, Charles opened the door to the den and stepped out, still yawning.

"Just as I suspected," Faith teased. "You *were* napping."

"I intended to revise the first chapter," he muttered, rubbing his eyes, "but the minute I sat down in that warm, quiet room, I was lost. Thank goodness there's a comfortable sofa in there or I would've fallen asleep with my head on the keyboard."

Faith had taken more than one nap in Emily's comfortable den, perhaps her favorite room in the house. In the early years, it had been Heather's bedroom, but as she grew up, Heather had wanted more privacy and claimed the room at the top of the stairs. Emily had transformed her daughter's former bedroom into a library, with books in every conceivable place. A desk and computer took up one wall, and the worn leather couch another. A hand-knit afghan was draped over its back for those times when reading led to napping…. She'd spent many a lazy winter afternoon on that couch, Faith recalled.

"What have you been up to?" Charles asked.

"I called Emily in Boston to see how she's doing," she told him.

Charles poured a mug of coffee. "Is she having any problems?"

"No. In fact, it seems your brother's decided to stay on."

"Stay on what?"

"In Boston with Emily."

Charles's eyes widened as he stared at her. "Let me see if I'm hearing you right. My brother didn't return to New York?"

"Nope." Faith loved the look of absolute shock. She wondered if Ray had shown the same degree of astonishment when he learned how well his brother had adjusted to Leavenworth and being with her.

"Has something happened in New York that I don't know about?" Charles asked.

"What do you mean?"

"Has the city been snowed in or has there been a train strike? That sort of thing?"

"Not that I've heard. I had the radio on earlier and they didn't mention anything. Why?"

"Why? Because my brother is a dyed-in-the-wool workaholic. Nothing keeps him away from his desk."

"Well, he's taking a few days off to spend with Emily."

Charles took a sip of coffee, as though he needed time to mull over what she'd told him. "Your friend must be one hell of a woman."

"She is." That was the simple truth.

Still distracted, Charles pulled out a kitchen chair and sat down. He glanced around and seemed to notice for the first time that she'd been busy. "You put up those decorations?"

"I didn't think you'd mind." She felt a bit uneasy about that now. Emily had a number of Christmas things she hadn't bothered to display this year; she'd obviously taken the rest of them to Boston. Faith had brought a few of her own decorations, as well. While everything was quiet, she'd unpacked the special ones and displayed them throughout the house. The tiny Christmas tree with red velvet bows stood on the mantel, and so did a small manger scene that Heather had loved since childhood. Emily's Christmas teapot, white china with holly decorations, now held pride of place on the kitchen counter.

Charles wandered into the dining room, Faith on his heels. "What's this?" he asked, motioning toward the centerpiece on the dining-room table.

"A cottonball snowman. Heather made it for Emily when she was eight. She was so proud of it, which is why Emily's kept it all these years."

Charles seemed puzzled, as if he couldn't quite grasp the beauty of the piece. Bells chimed softly from outside and Faith looked out the large picture window to see the horse-drawn sleigh gliding past.

"Charles, let's go for a sleigh ride," she said impulsively. For Faith, it was a highlight of the first and only Christmas she'd spent in Leavenworth—until now. It was the Christmas following her divorce. The sleigh ride, which she'd taken alone, had comforted her. That, and Emily's friendship, had made a painful Christmas tolerable, even pleasant. Her sleigh ride had shown her that being alone could bring its own contentment, its own pleasures. And spending Christmas Day with Emily and Heather had taught her that friendship could lend value to life.

Charles seemed startled by her invitation, then shook his head. "No, thanks."

"It's even more fun than sledding," she coaxed.

Still he declined.

"Well, come and stand in line with me while I wait my turn."

For a moment she thought he'd refuse, but then he nodded. "As long as the line isn't too long."

"Okay."

Dressed in their coats, boots, scarves and gloves, they strolled downtown, walking arm in arm. Night had settled over the small town, and festive activities abounded. The carolers in period costumes were out, standing on street corners singing. The Salvation Army band played Christmas music in the park, as ice skaters circled the frozen pond. Glittering multi-colored lights brightened the streets and the town was bustling with shoppers.

Fortunately, the line for the sleigh ride wasn't too long and while she waited, Charles bought them cups of creamy hot chocolate. "I'm so glad I remembered the sleigh ride," she said, holding her hot chocolate with gloved hands.

"Why's that?" Charles asked.

She shrugged, sipping at her chocolate. "I think I mentioned that I did my student teaching in Leavenworth—that's when I met Emily. Those months were hard on me emotionally. I'd only recently been divorced and I was feeling pretty bad. Before me, no one in my family had ever gotten a divorce."

"No one?"

"Not in my immediate family. My parents, grand-parents and sister were all happily married, and it really hurt my pride to admit that I'd made a mistake. I blamed myself because I hadn't listened when my parents warned me about Douglas."

"What happened?"

"My husband had a problem—he needed the approval and love of other women. Even now, I believe he loved me to the best of his ability, but Douglas could never be tied to a single woman."

"I see."

"I forgave him the first time he was unfaithful, although it nearly killed me, but the second time I knew this would always be a pattern with him. I thought—I hoped that if I got out of the marriage early enough, I'd be all right, but…I wasn't. I'm not."

Charles moved closer to her, and Faith looked down, tears blurring her eyes. She blinked them away and tried to compose herself, sipping the hot cocoa.

"Why aren't you all right? What do you mean?" he asked.

"I can't trust men anymore. I'm afraid of relationships. Look at me," she whispered. "Five years later, and I rarely date. All my dreams of marriage and family are gone and—" Resolutely she closed her mouth. What had possessed her to tell him this? "Listen," she told him, forcing a cheerful note into her voice, "forget I said anything."

Charles didn't answer right away. "I don't know if I can."

"Then pretend you have. Otherwise I'm going to feel embarrassed."

"Why should you?"

She shook her head. She hardly ever mentioned her divorce, not to anyone. Yet here she was, standing in the middle of this vibrant town in the most joyous season of the year, fighting back tears—spilling her heart to a man she hardly knew.

The sleigh glided up to the stop and the bells chimed as the chestnut mare bowed her head. The driver climbed down from his perch and offered Faith his hand. "Just one ticket," she said, about to give him the money.

"Make that two," Charles said, paying the driver. Without explaining why he'd changed his mind, he stepped up into the sleigh and settled on the narrow bench next to Faith.

The driver leaped back into the seat and took the reins.

Faith spread the woolen blanket over their laps. "What made you decide to come?" she asked.

He stared at her for a long moment. "I don't know... I just didn't want to leave you." He slid his arm around her shoulders and held her close. Warmth seeped into her blood. She hadn't realized how cold she was, but now Charles Brewster sat beside her in a one-horse open sleigh, two days before Christmas, and she felt warm, happy...and complete.

Chapter Twenty-Three

Emily woke the morning of Christmas Eve and stared up at the bedroom ceiling, musing that this was by far the most unusual Christmas of her life.

Not since the first Christmas following Peter's death had she dealt with such complex emotions during the holidays. For one thing, she'd been forced to acknowledge that Heather was an adult now, making her own decisions without the counsel of her mother.

As if *that* wasn't strange enough, Emily was in emotionally unfamiliar territory, living with a man she'd only known a few days. She sat up in bed and reviewed their time together. Ray was a hotshot New York publisher badly in need of a vacation, a career bachelor by all accounts. She was a widow and a small-town kindergarten teacher. Their meeting was accidental, as amusing as it was unexpected. They got along well, laughed together, and enjoyed each other's company. Much as she wanted to continue the relationship, Emily was realistic enough to accept that in a few days they'd both go back to their individual lives, three thousand miles apart. She decided then and there to make the most of their remaining time together.

After a quick shower, she dressed and emerged from the bedroom to discover that Ray was already up and reading the morning paper. The coffee was made. When she entered the kitchen, he lowered the newspaper and smiled.

"What's on the agenda for today?" he asked.

Emily wasn't sure. Back in Leavenworth, she'd be delivering charity baskets in the afternoon. Then, after a dinner of homemade clam chowder with Heather, followed by hot apple cider, she'd get ready for the Christmas Eve service at church. Home again, they'd go to bed, looking forward to a lazy Christmas morning, when they'd open their gifts and enjoy a late breakfast.

"I don't know what to do today," she said, feeling at a loss. "This year is completely unlike any I've ever experienced."

"What would you *like* to do?"

They'd spent their days sightseeing, and while Emily had thoroughly enjoyed this tour of American history, she wanted to concentrate on the season now.

"I'd like to bake cinnamon rolls," she said, coming to the decision quickly. "I do every year, specially for breakfast on Christmas morning. I think that would put me in the holiday spirit more than anything."

"Sounds fantastic. While you're doing that, I'll shop for our Christmas dinner. What shall we have?"

Emily shrugged. "A turkey might be a bit much for just the two of us."

"Didn't you say something about lobster earlier?" Ray asked.

She nodded, smiling. "Lobster would be perfect."

Emily must've realized she'd want to bake bread, because she'd tossed in a packet of yeast when she'd bought the supplies for her cookie baking venture. She began to systematically search the kitchen cupboards for bowls and pans.

When Ray finished reading the paper, he put on his overcoat. On his way out the door, he came into the kitchen, where Emily was busy assembling ingredients. The recipe was a longtime family favorite, one she knew by heart. Ray took her by the shoulders and turned her so she couldn't avoid looking at him.

"I know this Christmas isn't anything like you anticipated, and I'm sorry about that. But it's the best Christmas I've had since I was a kid—the year my dad got me the red racing bike I so desperately wanted."

"Oh, Ray," she whispered, "that's the nicest thing anyone's said to me in a long, long time." Unable to resist, she slipped her arms around his waist and hugged him. She hadn't been this intimate with a man in years, nor had she felt such longing. He didn't kiss her and, although she was disappointed, she applauded his restraint. There'd be time later to enjoy the sweetness of each other's company.

Whistling, Ray left the condo, and as soon as she'd mixed the dough, Emily set it in a slightly warmed oven to rise. Pulling on her coat, gloves and scarf, she hurried out the door. She wanted to buy Ray a Christmas gift and while she was at it, she needed to stop at the grocery store.

The weather was exactly as it should be: cold and clear, with snow falling lightly. Everyone seemed to be bustling about, intent on last-minute Christmas shopping. There was an infectious spirit of joy and goodwill wherever she went.

Ninety minutes later, when Emily returned to the condo, her arms were laden with packages and groceries. She hummed a Christmas carol as she waited for the elevator. She hoped Ray had returned, too, but when she walked inside, the condo was silent and empty.

As quickly as she could, she unloaded her packages, hung up her coat and hid Ray's present in the bedroom to be wrapped that afternoon. She turned on the gas fireplace, and gentle flames flickered over the artificial log. She went to the radio next, and an instant later, the condo was filled with the glorious sounds of holiday music.

Ray didn't come back for another hour; among his purchases was a couple of deli sandwiches. Emily had been so busy, she'd forgotten to eat breakfast and it was now well past lunchtime.

"I think I should probably put these lobsters in water," he said, setting a large box on the counter. He filled the sink. "Should I add salt?"

"Salt?"

"They live in salt water. They might need it."

"I don't think so." Emily was preoccupied with unwrapping the sandwiches. Not until she turned around did she notice two huge lobsters looking directly at her. "They're alive!" She felt sorry for them and while Ray carried their sandwiches to the table, she released the rubber bands holding their claws together. Poor things, it seemed a shame to keep them prisoner.

Ray got two cold sodas from the refrigerator. "I wasn't sure about getting live lobsters, but I figured I could always exchange them if you'd rather."

"Ah..." Emily was afraid to admit she'd never cooked a live lobster in her life. Nor had she ever eaten anything more than a lobster tail. "This should be...well, a challenge."

"We'll figure it out," Ray said.

Emily agreed. They were both hungry and didn't attempt conversation until they'd finished lunch. To all outward appearances, they were like a long-married couple anticipating each other's needs. Ray handed her a napkin, she gave him the pepper mill, all without exchanging a word.

"Since neither of us knows that much about cooking lobsters, perhaps I *should* exchange these for cooked ones," Ray suggested once they'd eaten.

"That might be best." She took their empty plates into the kitchen and let out a small cry.

"What?" Ray demanded.

"One of the lobsters is missing."

"What do you mean, missing?"

"There's only one in the sink."

"That's impossible."

"I'm telling you there's only one lobster in the sink."

Ray entered the kitchen and stared into the sink. "One of the lobsters is missing."

Emily placed her hand on her hip. "The editor's eye misses nothing," she teased.

"Where could it have gone?"

"That's for you to find out. I've got dough to knead." She moved to the oven and was about to remove the bowl when she felt something attach itself to her pant leg. Glancing down she saw the lobster.

"Ah...Ray." She held out her leg. "I found the lobster."

"I can see that." He squatted down and petted the creature's head as if it were his favorite pet.

"You might want to detach him from my pant leg."

Ray frowned. "How did the rubber band get off his claws?"

"Er...I took them off. It seemed cruel."

"I see."

"Ray, this is all very interesting, but I'd prefer not to be worrying about this lobster crawling up my leg." She was trying hard not to giggle.

"If you have any ideas on how to remove him, let me know."

Emily tried to shake her leg, but the lobster was firmly affixed. Ray started to laugh then, and she found it impossible not to join him.

"What are we going to do?" she asked between giggles.

"I don't know." Ray bent down and tugged at her

jeans, but the lobster wasn't letting go. "Maybe you should take off your pants."

"Oh, sure."

"I'm not kidding."

By then, they were nearly hysterical with laughter. Emily leaned against the kitchen counter, her hand over her mouth, tears running down her cheeks. Ray sat on the floor.

"You've got yourself quite a mess here."

"Just return me with the lobster." Emily could picture it now: Ray walking into the fish market, with her slung over his shoulder, the lobster dangling from her pant leg.

They burst into laughter again.

There was a knock at the door, and Ray, still laughing, left the room. It must be one of the neighbors, Emily supposed, someone else who lived on this floor. She went with Ray, not about to let him escape without helping her first. They had their arms around each other and were nearly doubled over with laughter when he opened the door.

An older woman stood on the other side, wearing a fur coat and an elaborate hat with a protruding feather. Cradled in the folds of her fur was a white Pomeranian. The dog took one look at Emily and growled.

"Ray!"

"Mother!"

After a few seconds' silence, he asked, "How did you get in?"

"Some nice young man opened the door for me." She glared at Emily. "And who's this?" Bernice Brewster demanded.

Ray looked at Emily and started laughing all over again. "Do you mean Emily or were you referring to the lobster?"

Chapter Twenty-Four

Faith hoped it would snow on Christmas Eve; to her disappointment the day was cold and bright, but there was no sign of snow. Charles had gone out on some errand, and she'd stayed home, her favorite Christmas CD playing as she flipped through Emily's cookbooks, looking for Christmas dinner ideas. Really, she should've thought about this earlier. Charles had suggested a roast, and she was beginning to think that was a good plan. Since she'd never made a turkey, she was a little intimidated by the prospect.

Sipping a cup of coffee, she read through one recipe after another, searching for inspiration. The more she read, the hungrier she got.

The phone rang, and she sighed, half wondering if

she should answer. It wouldn't be for her. Still, habit and curiosity demanded she pick up the receiver.

"Merry Christmas," she greeted the unknown caller.

"Mom?" a small quizzical voice returned.

"Heather?"

"You're not my mother," Heather cried.

"This is Faith."

"Faith!" Heather sounded beside herself. "What are you doing in Washington? Where's my mom?"

"I came to surprise your mother, only she isn't here."

"Mom's still in Boston?"

"Yes," Faith said. "Where are you?"

"Boston."

Faith frowned. "I thought you went to Florida with some guy on a Harley."

"I did, but we...we had a parting of the ways. Where's my mother?"

"She's staying in Charles Brewster's condominium. I don't have the address but I understand it isn't that far from the Harvard campus."

"Not Professor Brewster?"

"One and the same. Why?"

"You mean to say he's in Leavenworth, and you are, too?" Heather asked incredulously.

Faith smiled at the comedy of errors. "Yes. I arrived shortly after Charles did. I came with Santa and the elves and then—"

"Who?"

"Never mind, it's complicated. But listen, everything's fine. Charles has been absolutely marvelous about all of this. He agreed to let me stay here until my original departure date." Faith hated to think what might've happened if he'd insisted she leave. She might still have been at the airport, waiting for a stand-by seat.

"You're talking about *Professor* Brewster?"

"Yes. Professor Charles Brewster."

"You say he's been...marvelous?" Heather seemed genuinely surprised.

"Yes." In fact, he'd been more than that, but Faith wasn't about to share any of the details with Heather.

"He *isn't* marvelous," Heather insisted. "He gave my roommate a C when she worked hard on every assignment and studied for every test. Well, okay, she fell asleep in his class, but who can blame her? The guy's boring."

"I happen to think he's a fascinating man," Faith said sharply, "so please keep your complaints to yourself."

"Faith?" Heather said, her voice dropping. "Are you...interested in Dr. Brewster?"

"That's none of your business."

Heather gave a short, abrupt laugh. "You are! I don't believe it. Just wait until Tracy hears this. Does the professor feel the same way about you? No, don't answer that 'cause I'll bet he does." She laughed again, as if this was the funniest thing she'd heard in weeks.

"It isn't that amusing," Faith said, surprised by her need to defend Charles.

But Heather had already moved on to her own concerns. "So Mom's still in Boston," she said.

"Yes, she couldn't fly home without paying a high-priced penalty."

"That's wonderful." Heather sighed with relief. "Don't say anything to her, okay?"

"Yes, but there's something you—"

"I want to surprise her, so promise you won't say a word."

Faith leaned against the kitchen counter and raised her eyes to the ceiling, resisting the urge to laugh. "You have my word of honor. I won't let her know."

"Great. Thanks, Faith. Say hello to the professor for me."

"Sure."

"I'm going to be my mom's Christmas surprise." With that, Heather terminated the call.

Faith's smile grew. Heather was about to discover a surprise of her own.

Just then, the front door opened and Charles staggered into the house, his arms stacked high with packages. Blindly he made his way into the dining room, piling the festively wrapped gifts on the table. Bags hung from his arms, and he set those next to the boxes.

"Good grief!" Faith rushed forward to help him. "What have you done?"

"I went shopping." His smile was as bright as sun on snow. He looked downright boyish, with a swath of brown hair falling over his brow, his eyes sparkling.

"Who are all these gifts for?"

"The Kennedy kids get a bunch of them and there are a couple in here for you and..." He seemed decidedly pleased with himself.

"Charles." He resembled Scrooge the day after his nightmare, rushing about buying gifts. Faith half listened for Tiny Tim.

"I got something else for Emily, too, in appreciation for trading places with me."

This was quite a switch from his initial attitude. "The way I remember it, you said you'd walked into the middle of a Christmas nightmare." Faith couldn't restrain a smile. "And then I showed up."

"That was no nightmare," he said softly. "That was a gift."

Faith didn't know what to say. His intensity flustered her and she felt the heat rush into her cheeks.

After the sleigh ride, something had happened between them, something that was difficult to put into words. She sensed that sharing her pain and the bitter disappointment of her divorce had, in some strange way, released *him*. Charles hadn't said anything, but Faith realized words were often inadequate when it came to conveying emotions. She'd noticed the changes in him last night and even more so this morning.

"You got presents for the Kennedy kids?" she asked, pointing to the packages.

He nodded. "Did you know their dad got laid off last month?"

The kids hadn't said anything to her, but apparently they had to Charles.

"They didn't tell me, either," he told her before she could comment, "but I overheard Mark and Thomas talking about it. And then, early this morning, I saw someone deliver a food basket to the house. With six children, it's got to be tough this time of year."

"What a sweet thing to do. If you want, I'll help you write up gift cards and deliver them."

He nodded and the boyish, pleased look was back. "I enjoyed myself today. I didn't know Christmas could be this much fun. It's always been a time I dreaded."

"But why?"

Charles glanced away. "It's a long story, and a boring one at that."

"Involving a woman, no doubt."

He shrugged.

Faith waited expectantly. She'd shared her pain with him; the least he could do was trust her enough to divulge his.

"I see," she said after an awkward moment. She turned back to the kitchen.

Charles followed her. "If you want to know—"

"No, it isn't necessary," she broke in. "Really."

"It was a devastating experience, and I'd prefer not to discuss it."

"I understand," she said and she did. Faith reassured him with a smile, gathering up the cookbooks and replacing them on the shelf.

"Her name was Monica."

Faith pretended not to hear.

"I loved her and I was sure she loved me."

"Charles, really, you don't need to explain if you'd rather not."

He threw off his coat and sat at the table. "But I would. Please." He gestured to the chair across from him.

Faith pulled it out and sat down. He took her hands, holding them in his own. "I adored her and assumed she felt the same way about me. I bought an engagement ring and planned to give it to her on Christmas Day. Thankfully I never had the opportunity to ask her to marry me."

"Thankfully?"

Charles's fingers tightened around hers. "She told me on Christmas Eve that she found me dull and tedious. I learned later that she'd met someone else."

Faith knew he didn't want her sympathy and she didn't offer it. "I think she was an extremely foolish woman."

Charles raised his eyes until they met hers. "I *am* dull and tedious."

"No," she countered swiftly. "You're brilliant and absentminded and quite possibly the kindest man I know."

A slow smile touched his mouth. "And you," he said. "You're the most marvelous woman I've ever met."

Chapter Twenty-Five

"Alone at last," Ray muttered as he shut the condo door. He'd walked his mother outside and waited with her until the taxi arrived to take her to the Four Seasons Hotel.

"Ray!" Emily said. "Your mother is hilarious."

"Believe me, I know. She's also meddling and demanding."

"But she loves you and worries about you."

"I should be worrying about *her*," Ray said. "I can't believe she'd fly here without telling me."

"She tried," Emily reminded him. "If I remember correctly, she left four messages, none of which you returned."

Ray looked up at the ceiling and rolled his eyes. "Guilty as charged."

"She does have impeccable timing, though, doesn't she?" Emily doubted she'd ever forget the expression on Bernice's face when Emily appeared at the front door with a lobster attached to her pant leg. The Pomeranian had started barking like crazy, and pandemonium had immediately broken out. Bernice wanted answers and Emily wanted the lobster off her leg and the dog had taken an immediate dislike to both the lobster and Emily. FiFi had leaped out of Bernice's arms, grabbing hold of Emily's other pant leg, and she was caught in a tug-of-war between the lobster and the lapdog.

Everything eventually got sorted out, but until Ray was able to rescue Emily and assure his mother that all was well, it had been a complete and total circus.

"This isn't the way I intended to spend Christmas Eve," Ray said.

"It was wonderful," Emily told him. His mother had known exactly what to do with the lobsters and she'd taken over in the kitchen, issuing orders and expecting them to be obeyed. Ray and Emily had happily complied. That evening, the three of them had feasted on the lobsters and a huge Caesar salad.

After dinner, they'd gathered in front of the fireplace, sipping wine and listening to Christmas music, and Bernice had delighted Emily with tales of her two sons growing up. Emily had enjoyed the evening immensely. And while he might complain, Ray seemed to take pleasure in their visit with his mother, too.

"She insists on taking us out for Christmas dinner," Ray said.

"That would be lovely."

"I'll bet you've never eaten at a hotel on Christmas Day in your life."

"True, but nothing about this Christmas is normal."

Ray walked over to where she stood by the tree. "Do you mind sharing the day with my mother and me?"

Emily smiled. "I consider myself fortunate to be with you both." She was sorry she couldn't be with her daughter, but she'd come a long way since Heather had announced she wouldn't be flying home for the holidays. She was far more prepared to accept Heather's independence, for one thing; it was a natural, healthy process and it was going to happen anyway, so she saw no point in fighting it.

"You're right, this isn't the Christmas Eve I expected," she added, "but I've had such a fabulous time in Boston and I owe it all to you."

"I should be the one thanking you," he whispered, drawing her into his arms. His kisses were gentle but thorough, coaxing and sensual. Emily's knees were weak by the time he released her.

"I have something for you," he said, stroking her arms. He seemed unable to stop touching her, and Emily was equally loath to break away from him.

"I have something for you, too," she told him.

"Me first."

"Okay." They separated and went to their respective bedrooms to retrieve their gifts. A few minutes later, as they sat beneath the Christmas tree, he handed her a small beribboned box. Emily stared at the beautifully wrapped present and then at Ray.

"Open it," he urged.

Her pulse going wild, she tore away the red satin bow and the wrapping paper. The jeweler's box surprised her. This looked expensive.

"Ray?" Her eyes flew up to meet his.

"Open it," he said again.

Slowly, Emily lifted the lid and swallowed a gasp. Inside was a cameo, about the size of a silver dollar.

"It's on a chain," Ray said.

"I love cameos," she whispered, and wondered how he could possibly have known. "Did I mention that?" She had two precious cameos that were among her most treasured possessions. The first had belonged to her grandmother and the second, a small one about the size of a dime, held an even deeper significance. Peter had given it to her on their fifth wedding anniversary. Now she had a third.

"I didn't know, but I saw this one and somehow I was sure you'd like it."

"Oh, Ray, I do. Thank you so much."

He helped her remove it from its plush bed. Emily turned her back to him and lifted her hair so he could connect the chain. This cameo was the most perfect gift he could possibly have given her. The fact that he'd sensed, after such a short acquaintance, how much it would appeal to her, was truly touching.

"This is for you," she said shyly, handing him her present. The day before, they'd strolled past an antique store that specialized in rare books. That morning, she'd gone inside to investigate and discovered a first edition of the science fiction classic *Dune* by Frank Herbert. It was autographed, and because this was Christmas Eve, she'd been able to talk the dealer down to a reasonable price.

In one of their many conversations, Ray had said that he'd enjoyed science fiction as a teenager. She watched as he eagerly ripped off the paper. When he saw the novel, his eyes grew wide.

"It's autographed," she told him, smiling.

Ray's mouth sagged open. "I loved *Dune* as a kid. I read it so many times the pages fell out."

Reverently he opened the book. "How did you know?" The whispered question revealed his own astonishment that she could find him such a fitting gift.

"I listened."

"You listened with your heart." His fingertips grazed her cheek as his eyes held hers. Slowly he glided his hand around the nape of her neck and brought her closer to thank her with a kiss.

Emily opened her lips to his. Their kisses were warm, moist, each more intense than the one before. Ray leaned back, gazing at her for several breath-stopping moments. Then he wrapped his arms around her and held her hard against him.

"Ray?"

He answered her with another kiss, and any sensible thoughts she might have had vanished the moment his lips met hers. He lowered her to the carpet, leaning over her.

Emily slid her arms around his neck. Excitement tingled through her, and passion—so long dormant, so deeply buried—came to life.

Ray's hand cupped her breast and she gasped with pleasure. She was afraid and excited at the same time. He began to unfasten her blouse and when she saw that his fingers trembled, she gently brushed them aside and unbuttoned it herself. Just as she reached the last button, there was a knock at the door.

Ray looked at her. Startled, Emily looked at him. "Your mother?" she asked.

He shrugged and got to his feet. "I doubt it." He walked across the room. "Whoever it is, I'll get rid of them." From her vantage point, she couldn't see the door, but she could hear him open it.

Emily waited. At first nothing happened, and then she heard Heather's shocked voice.

"Who are you?"

"Ray Brewster. And you are?"

Heather sidestepped Ray and walked into the condo. Emily quickly bunched her blouse together and stared up at her daughter's horrified expression.

"Mother?" Heather screeched.

Emily was sure her face was as red as the lobster she'd had for dinner that very night.

Chapter Twenty-Six

When Faith woke on Christmas morning, it was snowing, just as she'd hoped. Tossing aside the covers, she leaped out of bed, thrust both arms into her housecoat and bounded down the stairs. Happiness bubbled up inside her—it was Christmas Day!

From their short time together, Faith knew Charles wasn't a morning person, but she couldn't bear to let him sleep in on a morning as special as this.

After putting on the coffee and waiting impatiently for enough of it to filter through to fill a cup, she swiftly removed the pot and stuck the mug directly under the drip. Then, coffee in hand, she walked down the hallway to the room in which Charles slept.

Knocking at the door, she called, "Wake up, it's Christmas! You can't escape me this morning."

She could hear him grumbling.

"Charles, it's *snowing!* Come on, get up now."

"What time is it, anyway?"

"Seven-thirty. I have coffee for you. If you want, I can bring it in."

"Do I have a choice?"

She laughed and admitted that he really didn't. If he chose to sleep longer, she'd simply rattle around the kitchen making lots of noise until he got up.

"All right, all right, come in."

He didn't sound too pleased, but Faith didn't care. When she creaked open the door, she discovered Charles sitting up in bed. His hair was disheveled and a book had fallen onto the floor.

"Merry Christmas," she said, handing him the coffee.

His stare was blank until he took his first sip. "Ahh," he breathed appreciatively. Then he gave her an absent grin. "Merry Christmas, Faith. Did Santa arrive?"

"Oh...I didn't think to look."

"Let me finish my coffee and shower, and then I'll take a peek under the tree with you."

"You're on," she said and backed out of the room before she could do something silly and completely out of character—like throw her arms around his neck and kiss him. With the two of them alone in Emily's cozy house, the atmosphere had become more and more intimate....

A half hour later, Faith had dressed and was frying bacon for their breakfast when Charles appeared. He wore a dress shirt and sweater vest.

"Merry Christmas!" he said again.

"You, too." She made an effort not to look at him for fear she'd be too easily distracted.

"So, did you check under the tree?" Charles asked.

"Not yet." She slid the bacon onto the platter and wiped her hands.

"You look very nice," Charles said. "I generally don't notice much of anything before ten. I don't know if it's the day or if it's you." His comment was as casual as if he were discussing the weather.

"Me?" she whispered.

"You're an attractive woman." He cleared his throat. "Very attractive."

"Oh."

"It's true."

Flustered now, she offered him a tentative smile. "Breakfast is ready." She carried the crisp bacon over to the kitchen table, which she'd already set using a poinsettia-covered tablecloth. The juice was poured and the toast made; scrambled eggs were heaped in a dish. A quiche lorraine sat in the center of the table. And she'd brewed fresh coffee, the aroma pervading the room. She'd prepared far more than the two of them could possibly eat, but she supposed the quiche would make a nice lunch tomorrow.

"I'm so glad it's snowing," she said excitedly.

"Why wouldn't it snow today? It's snowed every day since I got here."

"Not true," she countered, but then admitted he was right. It *had* snowed every day at some point. Watching the thick white flakes drifting down was a holiday ideal. She felt like a child again.

"Oh, my," she said, unaware that she'd spoken aloud.

"What?"

Faith shook her head, not wanting to answer. She realized that she'd forgotten what it felt like to be happy. It was as though a fog had lifted and the world had become newly vivid, the colors clear and pure. Her gaze flew across the table and she looked at Charles. She knew immediately that he was responsible for her change of attitude. Spending these days with him had opened her to the joy of the season and the promise of love. The divorce had robbed her of so much, shredded her self-confidence, undercut trust and faith and made her doubt herself. It had taken her a long time to deal with the loss, but she was stronger now. She could expect good things in her life. She could anticipate happiness.

"Faith?" he asked with a quizzical expression. "What is it?"

She glanced quickly away and dismissed his question with another shake of her head. "Nothing important."

"Then tell me."

She smiled. "I was just thinking how happy I am to be here, having breakfast with you on Christmas morning."

Charles let the comment rest between them for a long moment. "With me?"

She giggled because he sounded so shocked. "Yes, Charles, with you. Is that so strange?"

"As a matter of fact, yes. I'm not accustomed to anyone enjoying my company."

"Well, I do." She reached for an extra strip of bacon to create a distraction for herself.

Charles set his fork aside and sat back in his chair, staring across the table as if she'd taken his breath away.

Faith grew uncomfortable under his scrutiny. "What is it?" she demanded.

He grinned. "I was just thinking that I could love you."

"Charles!"

"This isn't a joke—I'm completely sincere. I'm halfway in love with you already. But I know what you're going to say."

"I'm sure you don't."

"Yes, I do," he insisted. "You're thinking it's much too soon and I couldn't possibly know my feelings yet. Two weeks from now, our encounter will be just a memory."

That *was* what she was thinking, although Faith badly wanted to stay in touch with Charles once they parted. But there was more to her reaction than that.

"I'm just so happy," she said, "and I realized I haven't been in a long time."

"Happy with me?"

She nodded.

"Could we...you know, call each other after the holidays?" He seemed almost afraid of her response.

"I'd like that."

His eyes sparkled with undisguised pleasure. "I was recently approached by Berkeley about a teaching position," he confided. "Is that anywhere close to you?"

"It's very close."

He took in that information with a slight nod. "Good. That's good."

The doorbell chimed, and Faith dropped her napkin on the table, rising to her feet. "I'll get it." She suspected it was one or more of the Kennedy kids, coming to thank Charles for the gifts. She wondered what he'd bought her; from all the hints he'd been dropping, she suspected it was something special. She'd found a small antique paperweight for him, and that, too, was under the tree.

When she opened the door, it wasn't the Kennedy kids she saw. Instead, there stood Sam with the six dwarfs crowding around him. The dwarfs looked as if all they needed was a word of encouragement before rushing inside and attacking Charles en masse.

"Sam!" she cried and was instantly crushed in a big hug.

"We came to check up on you," Tony said, peering inside the house.

"Yes," Allen added. "We wanted to make sure Scrooge was good to you."

"Everything's fine," she assured her friends, bringing them into the house—and bringing them up to date. By that time, Charles had joined them in the living room.

Santa's elves peered up at him suspiciously.

Tony took a step closer. "She said you've had an attitude adjustment. Is that true?"

Charles nodded, a solemn expression on his face. "Faith won me over."

Sam chuckled. "We thought we'd give you a ride back to Seattle, Faith, so you can catch your flight tomorrow afternoon."

"I'll drive her." Charles moved to her side, placing his arm around her shoulders.

"We're just finishing breakfast but there's plenty if you haven't eaten."

"We haven't," Sam said promptly, and the seven of them rushed into the kitchen.

"Can you stay for dinner?" Charles asked, surprising Faith with the invitation.

"No, no, we don't want to intrude. Besides, we have to head out soon for flights of our own. The only reason we came was to make sure everything was all right with Faith."

"I'm having a wonderful Christmas," Faith told her friends.

And I'm going to have a wonderful life.

Chapter Twenty-Seven

"I've never eaten at the Four Seasons in my life," Emily said anxiously, "Christmas or not." She was sure there'd be more spoons at a single place setting than she had in her entire kitchen.

"It's where Mother always stays when she's in town," Ray told her. His hand rested on the small of her back as he directed her into the huge and elegantly decorated hotel lobby, dominated by a massive Christmas tree.

Emily glanced around, hoping to see Heather. Her daughter had been shocked to find her and Ray together. Although mortified that Heather had caught her half-undressed—well, with her blouse unfastened, anyway—Emily had hurriedly introduced them. Then, summoning all the panache she could muster, she'd announced that she hadn't slept with him.

Her cheeks flamed at the memory of how she'd managed to embarrass all three of them in one short sentence.

"Do you see Heather?" Emily asked, scanning the lobby.

"No," Ray murmured, "but I'm not looking for her."

The two people she held so dear hadn't exactly gotten off on the right foot, and Emily blamed herself.

Ray had tried to explain that the condo actually belonged to his brother, Professor Brewster, but Heather had been too flustered and confused to respond. The scene had been awkward, to say the least. Complicating everything, Heather had immediately stumbled out.

She'd rushed after Heather to invite her to the hotel for Christmas dinner. Her daughter had pretended not to hear, then stepped into the elevator and cast Emily a disgusted look. She'd shaken her head disapprovingly, as if the last place on earth she wanted to be was with her mother and that...*man*.

Emily had gone back into the apartment with her stomach in knots. She still felt ill; her stomachache hadn't abated since last night and she'd hardly been able to force down any breakfast.

"She'll be here any minute," Ray told her.

"Do you think so?" Emily's voice swelled with anticipation and renewed hope.

Ray exhaled loudly. "Actually, I was referring to my mother."

"Oh." Her shoulders deflated.

"Heather will make her own decision," Ray said, giving her shoulder a reassuring squeeze.

"I know." Emily had already realized that, but it was hard not to call her and smooth things out, despite Heather's rude behavior. To be estranged from her only child on Christmas Day was almost more than Emily could bear. If she hadn't heard from her by early evening, she knew she'd break down and call.

"Rayburn!" His mother stepped out of the elevator, minus FiFi the Pomeranian. She held out her arms to her son as she slowly glided across the lobby. Several heads turned in their direction.

"Mother likes to make an entrance," Ray said under his breath.

"So I noticed."

Bernice Brewster hugged Ray as if it'd been years since their last meeting, and then shifted her attention to Emily. Clasping both of Emily's hands, the older woman smiled benevolently.

"I am so pleased that my son has finally found someone so special."

"Mother, stop it," Ray hissed under his breath.

Emily quite enjoyed his discomfort. "Ray's the special one, Mrs. Brewster."

"I do agree, but it takes the right woman to recognize what a prize he is."

"What time is the dinner reservation?" Ray asked in an obvious attempt to change the subject.

"Three-thirty," his mother informed him. "I do hope you're hungry."

"I'm famished," Emily said, although it wasn't true. Worried as she was about Heather, she didn't know if she could eat a single bite. "I, uh, hope you don't mind, but I invited my daughter to join us…. She didn't know if she could make it or not."

Ray gripped her hand at the telltale wobble in her voice.

"Is anything wrong, my dear?" Mrs. Brewster asked.

"I—Heather and I had a bit of a disagreement."

"Children inflict those on their parents every now and then." Ray's mother looked pointedly in his direction. "Isn't that right, Rayburn?"

Ray cleared his throat and agreed. "It's been known to happen. Every now and then, as you say."

"Don't you worry," the older woman said, gently patting Emily's forearm. "We'll ask the maître d' to seat us at a table for four and trust your daughter has the good sense to make an appearance."

"I hope she does, too."

Ray spoke to the maître d' and they were led to a table with four place settings. Emily was surprised by the number of people who ate dinner in a restaurant on Christmas Day. Aujourd'hui was full, with a long waiting list, if the people assembled near the front were any indication.

The maître d' seated Mrs. Brewster, and Ray pulled out Emily's chair. She was half seated when she saw Heather. Her daughter rushed into the restaurant foyer, glancing around the tables until she caught sight of Emily. A smile brightened her pretty face, and she came into the room, dragging a young man. It took Emily only a moment to recognize Ben.

Emily stood to meet her daughter.

"Mom!" Heather threw her arms around Emily's neck. "I'm so glad I found you."

Emily struggled with emotion. "I am, too." She could hardly speak since her throat was clogged with tears.

"Hi," Heather said, turning to Ray. She extended her hand. "We sort of met last night. I'm Heather."

Ray stood, and they exchanged handshakes. "Ray." He motioned to his mother. "This is my mother, Bernice Brewster."

"And this is Ben Miller," Heather said, slipping her arm around the young man's waist. She pressed her head against his shoulder, as if they were a longtime couple. Emily was curious about what had happened to Elijah No-Last-Name, but figured she'd learn the details later.

"Please," Mrs. Brewster said, gesturing to the table. "I would like both of you to join us."

Immediately an extra chair and place setting were delivered to the table, and not a minute later everyone was seated.

"This place is really something," Heather said with awe. "You wouldn't believe some of the roadside dumps I ate at while I was in Florida. Thanks so much for including us."

"It's good to see you again," Emily said, smiling at Ben.

The college student grinned, and answered Heather's unspoken question. "Your mother and Ray bought a Christmas tree from me a few days ago."

"Oh."

"When did you two…" Emily began, but wasn't sure how to phrase what she wanted to ask.

"When I left last night, I was pretty upset," Heather confessed, reaching for her water glass. She didn't drink from it but held onto it tightly. "I don't really know why I took off the way I did." She turned to Ray's mother. "I guess I didn't expect to find my mother with a man, you know?"

"Rayburn isn't just a regular run-of-the-mill man," Bernice said with more than a trace of indignation.

"I know—well, at first I didn't, but I'm over that now." Heather drew in a deep breath. "When I left the condo, I wasn't sure where to go or what to do, so I started walking and—"

"I saw her," Ben interrupted, "kind of wandering aimlessly down the street."

"You were still at the Christmas tree lot?" Ray asked.

Ben nodded. "For those last-minute shoppers. Technically I should've closed about an hour earlier, but I didn't have anywhere to be, so I stuck around."

"It was a good thing, too," Heather said, her eyes brimming with gratitude. "I don't know what I would've done without Ben."

"I closed down the lot, and then Heather and I found somewhere to have coffee and we talked."

"Ben told me just what I needed to hear. He said I was being ridiculous and that my mother was entitled to her own life."

The waiter appeared then, and handed everyone elegant menus. Heather paused until he'd finished.

"It's just that I never thought my mother would ever be interested in a man other than my father," she continued in a low voice as Bernice perused the wine list. "I was...shocked, you know?"

Beneath the table, Ray took Emily's hand and they entwined their fingers.

"You *are* interested in Ray, aren't you?" Heather asked her mother.

The entire room seemed to go silent, as though everyone was waiting for Emily's reply. "Well…"

Mrs. Brewster leaned closer. So did Ray.

"I—I guess you could s-say I'm interested," she stammered. Now that the words were out, she suddenly felt more confident. "As a matter of fact, yes, I am. Definitely. Yes."

Mrs. Brewster released a long sigh. "Is it too early to discuss the wedding?"

"Yes." Ray and Emily spoke simultaneously and then both smothered their laughter.

"We've just met," Ray reminded everyone. "Let's not get ahead of ourselves, okay?"

"But you are smitten, aren't you?" Ray's mother asked with such eagerness that Emily couldn't disappoint her.

"Very much," she said, smiling at the old-fashioned word.

"And Rayburn?"

"I'm smitten, too."

"Good." Mrs. Brewster turned to Heather next. "I think a pale green and the lightest of pinks for the wedding colors, don't you agree?"

Heather nodded. "Perfect."

"May or June?"

Heather sneaked a look at her mother and winked. "June."

Ray brought his head closer to Emily's and spoke behind the menu. "They're deciding our future. Do you object?"

Emily grinned, and a warm, happy feeling flowed through her. "Not especially. What about you?"

Ray grinned back. "I've always been fond of June."

"Me, too."

"My mother will drive us both crazy," he warned.

"I like her," Emily whispered. "I even like FiFi."

Ray studied Bernice and then sighed. "Mother *is* a sweetheart—despite everything."

The waiter approached the table. "Merry Christmas," he said formally, standing straight and tall, as if it was his distinct pleasure to serve them on this very special day of the year.

"May I offer you a drink to start off with?"

"Champagne!" Bernice called out. "Champagne all round."

"Champagne," the others echoed.

"We have a lot to celebrate," Bernice pronounced. "Christmas, a homecoming—and a wedding."

Epilogue

"This is so festive, isn't it?" Faith had seen pictures of Rockefeller Center, but that didn't compare to actually standing here, watching the skaters in their bright winter clothes. Some were performing elaborate twirls and leaps; others clung timidly to the sides. They all seemed to be having a good time.

"I knew you'd love it," Emily said.

"What I'd love to do is skate." Not that she would in what Charles referred to as her "delicate" condition. She rubbed her stomach with one hand, gently reassuring her unborn child that she wouldn't do anything so foolish when she was six months pregnant. In the other hand she held several shopping bags from Saks.

The two friends continued down the avenue,

weaving in and out of the crowd. Emily, too, carried packages and bags.

"I still can't imagine you living in New York City and actually loving it, especially after all those years in Leavenworth," Faith said. She was happy for Emily and Ray, but she'd been astonished when Emily had announced last spring that she was moving across the country.

"What I discovered is that New York is just a collection of small communities. There's Brooklyn and SoHo and the Village and Little Italy and Harlem and more."

"What about teaching? Is that any different?"

Emily shook her head. "Children are children, and the kindergartners here are just like the ones in Leavenworth. Okay, so they might be a bit more sophisticated, but in many ways five-year-olds are the same everywhere."

"What's new with Ray?"

Emily's lips turned up in a soft smile. "He works too hard. He brings his work home with him and spends far too many hours at the office, but according to everyone I've met, he's better now than ever."

"Better?"

Her friend blushed. "Happier."

"That," said Faith, "is what regular sex will do for you."

"Faith." Emily nudged her and laughed.

"It certainly worked with Charles."

"If you're going to talk about your love life, I don't want to hear it."

Faith enjoyed watching Emily blush. She'd never seen her this radiant. Life had certainly taken an interesting turn for them both, she reflected. Just a year earlier, they'd been lonely and depressed, facing the holidays alone. A mere twelve months later, each was married—and, to pile happiness on top of happiness, they were practically sisters now. Faith's baby was due in March, and Charles was about as excited as a man could get at the prospect of becoming a father.

His mother was pretty pleased with herself, too. Faith and Emily had both come to love Bernice Brewster. She'd waited nearly seventy years for daughters, and she lavished her daughters-in-law with gifts and occasional bits of motherly wisdom and advice. Well, perhaps more than occasional, but Faith had no objection and she doubted Emily did, either.

"When will Heather get here?" Faith asked, looking forward to seeing her.

"Tomorrow afternoon. She's taking the train down."

"How is she?"

Emily rearranged her shopping bags. "Heather's doing really well."

"Did you ever find out what happened with Elijah and the ill-fated Florida trip? I know she didn't want to talk about it for a while...."

Emily frowned. "Apparently he drank too much and he didn't like to eat in real restaurants. His idea of fine dining was a hot dog at a roadside stand. In addition to all that, he apparently had a roving eye, which Heather didn't approve of."

"That girl always was high maintenance," Faith teased. "What about her and Ben?"

"Who knows?" Emily said with a shrug. "She claims they're just friends but they seem to spend a lot of time together. Ben's going on to law school after graduation."

"Good for him."

"He might come down and spend Christmas with us, too."

"You'll have a houseful, with Heather and maybe Ben." Despite the invitation to spend Christmas in New York at their apartment, Charles and Faith had booked a room at the Warwick Hotel. Bernice was due to arrive, as well. She, of course, would be staying at the Plaza.

Faith doubted there was anyplace more romantic than New York at Christmastime.

She and Emily walked into the Warwick and down the steps to the small lobby. Ray and Charles stood when they came into the room. Even now, after all these months, Faith's heart fluttered at the sight of her husband. His eyes brightened when he saw her. The unexpected happiness she'd discovered last Christmas had never left. Instead, it had blossomed and grown. She was loved beyond measure by a man who was worthy of her devotion.

"Looks like you bought out Saks Fifth Avenue," Charles said as he took the packages from her hands.

"Just the baby department, but Charles, I couldn't help myself. Everything was so cute."

"Buying anything is a big mistake," Ray told them, helping Emily with her shopping bags. "Mother's waited all these years to spoil her first grandchild. My guess is she has stock in Toys 'R' Us by now."

"Don't forget a certain aunt and uncle, too," Emily murmured.

Faith wrapped her arm around Charles's and laid her head against his shoulder.

Emily read her perfectly. "Listen, why don't you two go to your room and rest for a little while? Faith needs to put her feet up and relax. Ray and I will have a drink and catch up. Then, when you're ready, we'll go out for dinner."

Faith nodded, grateful for her friend's sympathy and intuition.

Charles led the way to the elevator. He didn't speak until they were inside. "You overdid it, didn't you?"

"Only a bit. I'll be fine as soon as I sit down with a cup of herbal tea."

Her husband tucked his arm protectively around her and waited until they were back in the room to kiss her.

Then he ordered tea.

"Did you two have a chance to visit?" Ray asked as Emily removed her coat and slung it over the back of her chair. They'd entered the bar, securing a table near the window. "Or was shopping at the top of your priority list?"

"Actually, we did some of both. It's just so good to see Faith this happy."

The waitress came by, and Ray ordered a hot buttered rum for each of them.

"I can't believe the changes in her," Emily said. "She's so much more confident."

"I was going to say the same thing about Charles," her husband said with a bemused grin. "I hardly recognize my own brother. Until he met Faith, all he cared about was history—in fact, I think he would've preferred to live in the eighteenth century. I feel like I finally have a brother again."

The waitress brought their drinks and set them on the table, along with a bowl of salted nuts.

"Do you suppose they're talking about us in the

same way?" Emily asked. "Are we different people now than we were a year ago?"

"I know I am," Ray said.

"I think I am, too."

Emily reached for a pecan, her favorite nut, and then for no discernible reason started to laugh.

"What's so funny?"

"Us. Have you forgotten the day we met?"

Ray grinned. "Not likely."

"I was so miserable and upset, and then you happened along. I glommed on to you so fast, I can only imagine what you must've thought."

"*You* glommed on to me?" he repeated. "That's not the way I remember it." Ray grabbed a handful of nuts. "As I recall, I found out that my brother had traded homes with this incredibly lovely woman. The explanation was reasonable. All I had to do was reassure my mother everything was fine and catch the train back to New York."

Emily lowered her eyes and smiled. "I'm so glad you ended up staying."

"You think I missed the last train by accident?"

"You didn't?"

"Not by a long shot. As my mother would say, I was smitten. I still am."

"That's comforting to hear."

"Christmas with you last year was the best of my life."

"Except for the Christmas you got the red racer."

"Well, that was my second-best Christmas."

"And this year?"

"When Christmas comes, I'll let you know."

"You do that," Emily whispered, raising her glass in a toast to the most wonderful Christmas gift of her life.